D0919848

BOMBAY BRIDES

BOMBAY BRIDES

Esther David

HarperCollins *Publishers* India

First published in hardback in India by
HarperCollins *Publishers* in 2018
A-75, Sector 57, Noida, Uttar Pradesh 201301, India
www.harpercollins.co.in

2 4 6 8 10 9 7 5 3 1

P-ISBN: 978-93-5277-945-1
E-ISBN: 978-93-5277-946-8

This is a work of fiction and all characters and incidents described in this book
are the product of the author's imagination. Any resemblance to actual persons,
living or dead, is entirely coincidental.

Esther David asserts the moral right
to be identified as the author of this work.

Typeset in 12/15 Arno Pro at
Manipal Digital Systems, Manipal

Printed and bound at
Thomson Press (India) Ltd.

MIX
Paper
FSC   FSC® C010615

This book is produced from independently certified FSC® paper to ensure
responsible forest management.

To Grandmother Shebabeth – one of the first few 'Bombay Brides' who came to Ahmedabad.

Contents

Author's Note

SINCE 1994, I have been writing books based on the theme of the Jewish experience in India. My novels are about the diminishing community of Indian Jews. Since the mid-1960s, many Jewish families have emigrated to Israel and other countries. Those who have chosen to live in India are not sure if they should leave for Israel or stay on. So I write about cross-cultural conflicts and the isolation experienced by them. My novels probe the concepts of home and roots.

Almost all my novels are set in Ahmedabad. I created the fictional Shalom India Housing Society in Ahmedabad in 2005.

In *Bombay Brides*, I have woven narratives around the Bene Israel Jews of Ahmedabad living in this society. I decided on the title 'Bombay Brides' as most Jewish men of Ahmedabad are married to women from Mumbai and these stories are woven around their lives. While writing this book, I often visited Jewish homes and observed their lifestyles in Ahmedabad, Mumbai, Alibaug, Cochin and Kolkata.

Writing about Jewish life has helped me understand my community, the Bene Israel Jews of western India, which has held on to its roots in India. The Bene Israelis continue to preserve their heritage, rites and rituals in an Indian environment. *Bombay Brides* tries to capture the emotional crisis faced by the last surviving Jews in a vast multi-cultural country like India. The focus is on Juliet's empty apartment at Shalom India Housing Society. After Juliet and Romiel get married, they leave for Israel. They stay there for five years, periodically renting out their apartment A-107, preferably to Jews. Each character has a story, which is connected to the other residents of the housing society. Prophet Elijah, in whom the Bene Israel Jews believe, plays an important role here. Mischievously, he often creates havoc in the lives of the residents, appearing at some critical or amusing moment, but ultimately makes sure that peace prevails.

Who is Prophet Elijah?

THE BENE ISRAEL Jews of India have a great fascination for Prophet Elijah, also known as Eliahu Hannavi. The Prophet appears in several stories in the Torah—Kings I-II. The story of his ascension to heaven in a chariot of fire is connected to the belief that he will herald the Messiah's arrival on earth.

The Bene Israel Jews believe that the Prophet rose to heaven from a site near Haifa in Israel, passing through India. His chariot touched a rock in Khandala, a small village near Alibaug on the Konkan coast in Maharashtra, where members of the community make vows to fulfil their wishes. Once the wish is fulfilled, a malida is offered to Prophet Elijah with a plate of flaked rice mixed with grated coconut, dates and fruit. Often, the malida is followed by a community dinner. For Bene Israel Jews, all rituals begin with a prayer to him. Perhaps the Bene Israel elders of ancient times created the cult of Eliahu Hannavi to keep the community together.

All over the world, in Jewish homes, Prophet Elijah has special significance during the seven-day festival of Passover. It is believed that he visits their homes, and a special chair and goblet of wine are kept for him on the Seder table.

1

Juliet

JULIET ABRAHAM IS our first Bombay bride.

Abraham, a Mumbai-based Jew, had recently shifted to Ahmedabad with his wife Rebecca, daughter Juliet and son Abner. Abraham had been transferred as the branch manager of a well-known company of home appliances. Even before they had settled down in their company apartment at Citizen Flats near Satellite Crossroads, Juliet fell in love with Rahul.

Juliet and Rahul met at a catering college in Ahmedabad. Both had a passion for food, which they wanted to turn into a profession. Juliet had become well-known in the Jewish community of Ahmedabad for winning prizes at cooking contests. Her victories were celebrated with parties, to which she often invited Rahul.

But when Rebecca caught Rahul kissing Juliet on the landing of their building, she decided that Juliet had to be married off immediately to a good Bene Israel Jewish boy. She was worried that her daughter would elope with Rahul. How would she then face the community? She was always showing off about how her daughter was not only beautiful, but also talented. They had a reputation of being God-fearing Jews and Juliet had been brought up with the values of Judaism. From a young age, she had religiously followed all rituals and was known to be a 'good' girl. So they were sure that it was Rahul who was evil and had led her astray. Maybe she was no longer a virgin. Her mother started counting the days of Juliet's menstrual cycle. She blamed herself for allowing her daughter to spend so much time with Rahul.

Rebecca also heard from her neighbours that Rahul used to be in and out of their apartment on the pretext of exchanging notes, books or music. He was from Bhavnagar in north Gujarat and stayed in a hostel, so Juliet would often invite him home for lunch or dinner or to watch a cricket match on television with her family. Initially, her parents had been amused by the fact that Juliet's father's name was Abraham while Rahul's family name was Abhiram.

Rebecca drummed into Juliet that she was Jewish and had to follow the Law by getting married to a Jewish man and increasing the tribe. She wrote to a Jewish matchmaker in Mumbai and asked him to find a groom. But Prophet Elijah had other plans.

After innumerable discussions, arguments and fights, Juliet's parents found a solution to their problem. They sent her to Israel in Rebecca's cousin Hannah's custody. But with Abner's help, Rahul tracked Juliet down and phoned her. While she was speaking to Rahul, Juliet noticed that Aunt Hannah, who had been told about him by Juliet's parents, did not seem to be particularly angry with her. Instead she asked, 'Was that Rahul? You don't have to hide it from me.'

Juliet was surprised that Aunt Hannah was sympathetic and that she could trust her. So she said, 'Aunty, I am in love with Rahul.'

'I know. Your parents have told me everything. Well, this is the curse of belonging to a minority community.'

'Why do you say that?'

Aunt Hannah smiled ruefully. 'I was also in love with someone else, but was forced to marry your uncle. Fortunately, he is a good man and I came to terms with my life. So if you love Rahul, why don't you make your life with him?'

Hesitantly, Juliet asked, 'Aunt Hannah, will you help us?'

'Yes, but let me warn you, once you take the final step, neither community will accept you or your children.'

'So, what should I do?'

'Convert.'

'How... I know Rahul likes Israel and would like to work here as a chef.'

'I suggest that you convince Rahul to convert to Judaism. That will be the easiest. It takes longer in Israel, as he would have to study the Torah and even undergo a circumcision. I am told it is faster in India.'

Juliet sat huddled on the sofa, biting her nails. 'What if Rahul does not agree?' she asked.

'Then you could become a Hindu. But I suggest you ask him to convert and settle in Israel. You said he wants to start a restaurant. Indian restaurants do very well here. Look at the tandoori place in Tel Aviv.'

Juliet was not sure how Rahul would react to such a suggestion. After all, he had obligations to his family. They would never agree to their son converting to a strange religion like Judaism.

Six months later, Rahul travelled to Israel with a company that had an exchange programme with a kibbutz for trainee chefs. On arrival, he called Juliet and told her that he was in Israel. She was very excited and wanted to meet him that very day. But Aunt Hannah stopped her, as her husband Uncle Rahmim would not approve. He was sending reports about Juliet by email to her father every day. He was also very conscious of upholding the family's honour and had decided that his nephew, Ralphi, would be the perfect groom for his niece. Ralphi's family had been looking for a good Bene Israel bride for their son.

Juliet's parents happily agreed to the alliance. They distributed sweets, telling everybody that Juliet was soon to be married and they were flying to Israel for her wedding.

Juliet told Aunt Hannah she could not possibly marry Ralphi. She wept. 'I love Rahul, not Ralphi.'

Aunt Hannah looked deep into her eyes and whispered, 'Go, find him.'

Hannah and Juliet had to plan carefully so that Uncle Rahmim did not grow suspicious about their occasional outings. Aunt Hannah accompanied Juliet when she met Rahul at the Tel Aviv bus terminus after six months. They hugged, kissed and did not want to part.

That month, Rahul and Juliet met often, but always with Aunt Hannah chaperoning. Whenever they met, Aunt Hannah tried to convince Rahul to convert; it would be easier for them to get married.

Rahul liked Israel and enjoyed his stay at the kibbutz. The Israeli atmosphere had gone to his head and he had become fearless and bold. He was willing to brave all odds for his love.

Eventually, Aunt Hannah bought an airline ticket to India for Juliet and made all the preparations for their runaway marriage. Rahul already had a return ticket.

An old friend of Aunt Hannah was to receive them in Mumbai and arrange for a civil marriage, after which Rahul would have a meeting with the cantor of a synagogue in the suburbs and start the process of conversion. It would take three months.

On their departure, Aunt Hannah gave them a cheque to help them in the initial difficult days.

As they kissed her goodbye, Aunt Hannah blessed them, asking Prophet Elijah to protect them from all difficulties.

In Mumbai, it was easier than expected. They got married and called and informed their parents. At first, both families were furious, but then came together to receive the young couple at the Ahmedabad railway station. Aunt Hannah's plan worked. Both families welcomed them back with open arms. If Rahul's parents were disturbed about his decision to convert, they did not say anything.

Despite their misgivings, Juliet's and Rahul's parents organized a grand wedding reception at a five-star hotel and invited relatives and friends from both communities. This was when they were given new names to begin their journey into wedded life, Romiel–Rahul and Juliet–Priya.

Standing on the flower-bedecked dais, the young couple greeted their Hindu relatives by touching their feet and shook hands with their Jewish guests. Between the welcome aarti for the bride and groom, the wedding march and the cake-cutting ceremony, Abraham and Abhiram announced that they had bought an apartment for the couple at Shalom India Housing Society on Satellite Road.

The residents of Block-A of the housing society loved the young couple. They made Rahul feel like he was one of them. They often teased the two, referring to them as Romeo and Juliet, and said that Abhiram sounded like Abraham, so how did it matter if Romiel was actually Rahul? They invited Rahul's family for malida ceremonies and other festivities and even asked Rahul's mother to bring Gujarati snacks for the community dinner.

That was when Prophet Elijah intervened, as he had heard Juliet's prayers calling out to him, asking him to help decide their future.

Rahul and Juliet decided to emigrate to Israel, and Rahul's parents were invited for a malida as thanksgiving to Prophet Elijah. Rahul's father wore a kippa cap and his mother pinned a handkerchief on her head, just like a Bene Israel Jewish woman.

On the eve of their departure, Rahul–Romiel and Juliet–Priya left the keys of their flat with Ezra, the builder-cum-president of Shalom India Housing Society, asking him to sell the flat for them, as they would need the money in Israel.

When Ezra built the society, he had decided that Block-A would only be allotted to Jews. He advised Juliet to rent out the apartment to Jews who often came to Ahmedabad for a year or two, so that she would have some extra income.

Juliet agreed.

That is why this narrative is woven around Romiel and Juliet's apartment A-107 at Shalom India Housing Society.

2
Maa Myramayi

Myra came to Ahmedabad as a volunteer on an American programme of Torah studies for Indian Jews. She had earlier met Ezra when he had gone to America for a World Jewish Congress. She had never come across an Indian Jew and was fascinated that there were Jews in India, in a place called Ahmedabad. She was also amazed that they had a synagogue. Like most foreigners, she knew about Mumbai, but had never heard of Ahmedabad. She worked in a Jewish social centre and was well versed in the Torah, so she wondered if she could visit India on an educational programme for Jews. She knew of many Jewish groups that could sponsor her trip. Ezra immediately invited her to Ahmedabad.

Myra had never been to India, so she asked Ezra innumerable questions about the country. Ezra patiently answered them while he studied the petite woman. He tried to guess her age. He thought she was somewhere between thirty and forty, maybe younger, but because her face was haggard, it was hard to tell. She had a thin face, long nose, fuzzy red hair and large violet eyes that looked eternally surprised.

With the possibility of her coming to India, Ezra started fantasizing about Myra and having a torrid affair with her. He noticed that she had a nice body with small, taut breasts. He knew he was on religious duty in America and should not have pagan thoughts, but it was hard to break old habits, like having imaginary romances.

Myra appeared to be single. But one never knew when a boyfriend might appear. How did it matter? She was discussing her trip, asking where she could stay and other details.

Without thinking twice or wondering what his wife Sigaut or the community would have to say in the matter, he suggested that she stay in Juliet's flat. He said it on the spur of the moment, without consulting Juliet. He told himself that it did not matter, as the flat was empty. It was unfurnished, but then the inhabitants of Shalom India Housing Society were kind and would be sure to help.

'No problem,' he said, smiling and wondering how he would cheat on his wife with Myra.

Ezra assumed that his dream would come true when Myra would eventually come to Ahmedabad and set up home in Juliet's apartment. Juliet agreed to rent out her flat on the condition that Myra pay her two months' rent in advance, in dollars, in Israel. She also sent specific instructions that Myra pay the electricity bill and not disclose that she was a tenant, due to municipal tax problems. Myra agreed to all the terms and sent the rent to Israel. Juliet was happy with the arrangement.

Although Ezra had requested Salome, who along with her husband Daniyal was a caretaker of the society, to set up the apartment for

Myra, he realized from day one that it was not going to be easy to realize his dream of an extra-marital affair, for Salome was always present in Myra's flat. To add to his woes, the residents of the society pooled everything extra that they had—like mattresses, pillows, a table, two chairs, a small cupboard, a quilt, an assortment of dishes and cutlery—and lent it all to Myra. Juliet's mother gave her a gas cylinder and their old fridge, so all Myra had to buy was a stove, bed sheets, pillow covers, provisions and a printed tablecloth for her desk.

Myra and Salome installed old packing cases into a seating arrangement, which Myra covered with a block-print bedcover. Salome also offered to send a simple lunch of boiled vegetables, dal, rice and chapattis every day for five hundred rupees a month. Besides, Myra kept getting invites for lunch or dinner by one family or another, including Ezra's. He had boasted to Sigaut that he had invited Myra to teach the Torah at the synagogue, so he felt that it was his duty to invite her for Sabbath dinner. But when Myra attended the Sabbath service at Ezra's house, he was nervous and uncomfortable around her in Sigaut's presence.

Ezra rarely found Myra alone. Whenever he escaped Sigaut's vigilant eyes and rang Myra's doorbell to discuss the Torah study classes he had planned at the synagogue, Salome was always there. Or somebody stopped him when he was on his way to Myra's flat, needing help or advice, and he felt awkward ringing her doorbell in their presence. Eventually, Ezra gave up. He was sure that the housing society was conspiring to keep him away from her.

To find a way out, Ezra decided to have meetings with Myra at the synagogue office. This meant a drive down to the synagogue in his car and during the half-hour ride, he could be alone with her.

When they reached the synagogue, they would discuss details of classes and subjects. He suggested that she teach the Torah in the main prayer hall on weekends, when most people would be free. They also discussed the important question of English as the language of instruction, as most Bene Israel Jews found it difficult to follow Myra's accent and normally spoke in Marathi or Gujarati. They registered for the classes out of curiosity but then sat there staring blankly into space. To add to their problems, the Hebrew words were like Greek and Latin to them. Yet, they made an effort to follow Myra's rendition of the Torah.

Ezra was a busy man, but so great was his desire to befriend Myra that he volunteered to work as an interpreter. After all it was only for two months, he argued with himself. He knew that the number of people who came for the classes would dwindle with time and he would be left alone with Myra. He dreaded that Sigaut or Salome might join the Torah classes and was relieved that they did not, as they were busy when Myra held the classes.

Ezra would smile victoriously whenever he drove Myra to the synagogue. He would listen to her version of the Torah and after each session have discussions over tea and biscuits. Then he would drop her at the society and stop for a moment at his own place before going to the society office, so that Sigaut did not become suspicious.

For Ezra, this was an excellent arrangement. He had never been unfaithful to Sigaut and although he met Myra every day, he did not know how to get close to her. He was always afraid of being caught red-handed. What if he did manage to get intimate with Myra and at that very moment, Salome or someone else rang the doorbell?

The thought sent shivers down his spine.

'Coward,' he scolded himself.

Ezra's chase became futile when Myra joined a yoga class during the weekdays when she was not teaching at the synagogue. He was no longer sure if he had done the right thing by inviting her to India. To attend the yoga class, Myra would wake up as early as 4 a.m., sit in meditation and leave at 5 in an autorickshaw for the class. Ezra was disappointed that she had given up her Western clothes and was almost always dressed in salwar-kameez with a dupatta covering her head.

Ezra's plans were further jeopardized when Salome informed him that a young man who wore a tracksuit and sport shoes often dropped Myra at the society gate. Salome said that he was her yoga instructor.

Jealous, Ezra discreetly asked the security guard if the young man ever went up to Myra's flat. He felt reassured when he was told that the man never got off the scooter; he only dropped Myra at the gate, waved and drove off.

Soon, Salome was not going as frequently to Myra's apartment as before because whenever she rang the bell, Myra was either sitting in the Padmasan pose with eyes closed or in Shirshasan, the upside-down position, or watching a DVD of the guru's sermon on her laptop. But later Myra would always go down to Salome's flat, have tea with her and explain how she was discovering the spiritual side of India.

Myra was full of praise for the guru who ran the yoga centre, saying that though he was almost a hundred years old, because of yoga, meditation, fasting and simple vegetarian food he looked forty, and his face shone with an inner light.

Myra was fascinated by the guruji who gave her special discourses in English on Vedanta. The guru in turn was impressed that she was a highly educated religious American. Myra started spending long hours with him and Ezra rarely saw her. But she gave Ezra no reason to complain, as she was still diligent about her Torah classes. She told him politely that she would get to the synagogue on her own.

Every afternoon, she would arrive in an autorickshaw but sometimes the young instructor would drop her at the traffic light near the synagogue. In her simple salwar-kameez with a dupatta around her head, Myra looked so holy that Ezra stopped going to the synagogue and requested Lebana to help her with the translation. In fact, he was relieved to return to his routine: early-morning sessions at the laughing club, then his building construction office, home for a late lunch and a nap, and then attending to the problems of Shalom India Housing Society.

Ezra knew that Myra was a hot topic of discussion in the society. He often came upon women of the Jewish community standing in the foyer of the synagogue discussing her, her young yoga instructor and how she had distanced herself from the Jewish community. She no longer accepted their invitations for lunch, dinner or Sabbath, citing one excuse or another.

Salome informed the women that Myra's apartment was full of books on Vedanta and the Gita. Myra had made it clear to her that she did not like to be disturbed at odd times, as she meditated and would not open the door. She also stopped the lunch arrangement with Salome, saying that she now ate at the ashram.

With Myra's new-found interest in Indian philosophy, the Torah classes were no longer interesting, instead becoming long-winded and boring. When the participants complained, Ezra was embarrassed, but did not know how to tackle Myra, as she always got away by giving him a quote from the Gita.

Then one morning as Ezra was preparing to leave for the laughing club, the doorbell rang. Myra was standing outside. If it hadn't been for the colour of her hair, he would not have recognized her. She was wearing a white sari with a full-sleeved blouse and had her head covered. She greeted him with a namaskar instead of a handshake. Taken aback, he invited her in and asked Sigaut to bring her a cup of tea. Myra refused, saying that she was fasting. She wanted permission to take a week's leave from the Torah classes, as her yoga instructor had invited her for a trip to Jaisalmer. Ezra agreed enthusiastically and cancelled the Torah classes for a week. He was amused and wondered if she would go on a camel safari in a sari.

On her return, Myra came up with another demand. She had organized a satsang at her flat and invited a few people from the ashram. She wanted to make sure that there was no objection from Ezra. She saw the look on his face and explained hurriedly that satsangs were held at every member's house in turn each week and that week she had to organize one in her apartment. The guru never went to the homes of devotees, but was honouring her by visiting her.

'It is like a small party,' she explained. 'We will have group meditation followed by bhajans, after which I will serve fruit and milk to the satsangis.'

Ezra was taken aback and told her that he would have to ask the executive committee of the society. He did not want to take this decision on his own. That evening he called a meeting, saying that the committee's decision would be final. He asked Myra to be present and convince them.

Myra charmed the committee. She had worn jeans with a short kurti and won them over with her articulate explanation about the satsang. The committee gave her permission on the ground that the people of Shalom India Housing Society often held parties. Anyway, it did not matter, as she was returning to America in fifteen days. They were even planning a farewell party for her.

On the day of the satsang, Ezra was shocked when a car drew up at the society gates. A tall bearded man dressed in a dhoti, his shoulders covered with a shawl, stepped out. Myra received him by touching his feet and led him to her flat. Then a group of men and women arrived in a minibus and went up to her flat. Nobody would have known what happened in the flat after that, but Myra made one mistake. She asked Salome to help with the arrangements.

Later, Salome told her rapt audience at Shalom India Housing Society, 'Since joining the yoga classes, Myra had become rather distant with me. But when she decided to hold the satsang at her flat, she came to see me at lunchtime. Luckily, Daniyal was not at home and I offered her a plate of dal and rice. She accepted, saying that she had missed lunch at the ashram. She was dressed in shorts and a T-shirt with her bright red hair piled up on her head. When I complimented her, she thanked me, saying that she was cleaning the flat. She wanted my help to get durries, paper napkins, plates, spoons and glasses for the satsang. She also wanted me to prepare plates of fruit and kesar milk. I agreed and gave her an estimate of the cost. She accepted, although I had doubled my price. Then she went back, saying that she still had to fill the clay lamps with oil.

'That day, Myra spent a few hours at the synagogue. In the evening, as the lift was not working, I was climbing the stairs to Sippora's flat when I saw her dressed in a green silk sari with gold jewellery, a shiny bindi, and flowers in her hair. She looked the opposite of Myra the ascetic. She had made a star-shaped rangoli at her doorstep and decorated it with diyas. I stopped for a moment to admire her handiwork and invited her to join us at the synagogue for a malida. She refused, saying that Guruji had sent a car for her and she was leaving for Laxmi Puja at the ashram. She had the diyas outside her door for all the five days of Diwali. I know, I know, some of us also make rangoli, light diyas and burst crackers during Diwali, in keeping with the festive mood. We visit friends and offer sweets and on Dusshera, we like to eat fafda-jalebi and decorate our vehicles with flowers. But she seemed to take it a bit too seriously.

'A few days later, Myra and I went shopping for her satsang meeting. On the day of the satsang, I dressed in a white sari, out of respect for Myra's feelings. When I rang the doorbell of her flat, she opened the door and I saw that she had transformed from a smart

American woman into a demure satsangi in a white sari and long-sleeved blouse.

'Assuming there was a lot of time, I sat in her drawing room, peeling the fruit. Myra's brow furrowed, so I smiled and assured her that as soon as the guests arrived, I would move into the kitchen. She was apologetic and invited me to join the satsang. I refused, saying that I would be more comfortable in the kitchen.

'Overnight, Myra had hung a curtain at the kitchen door so that I could not see what was going on in the main room. I was going to charge her double the price for everything, so what did it matter? She forgot that I have ears and good eyesight. Moreover, her planning did not work. When she went downstairs to receive Guruji, she forgot the keys to the house. So she had to ring the bell. When I opened the door, she looked embarrassed as she led Guruji into the house and did not introduce me, as though I was her maidservant.

'A little stung, I went back to the kitchen, telling myself that I would triple the price.

'Later, I saw and heard a lot from the kitchen. The guru and Myra were sitting on chairs, while the rest were seated on the floor, eyes closed. When all the ceiling fans were switched on and the curtain moved, I saw that Guruji was seated just under the picture of Prophet Elijah. Strangely, they resembled each other, but for their clothes. The guru was wearing white. He had arrived in a car, while our Prophet was in a pink kaftan and riding a chariot of fire. The Prophet appeared to be shooting out of the guru's head. Somehow, I got the impression that they were flying away together in a chariot. Guruji looked younger than Maa Myramayi. I also recognized the young yoga instructor in the group of devotees. He looked different in a white kurta. I have never been able to figure out if she is closer to the young instructor or to Guruji.

'They were all chanting a prayer when the guru asked them to start the group meditation. There was pin-drop silence, so much so that I was afraid to move. As I still had to prepare the milk, I closed the kitchen door and stirred it in a huge vessel I had borrowed from Elisheba.

'They meditated for half an hour, during which I had to move noiselessly. When the guru gave the signal that the meditation was over, there was a question-and-answer session. All the questions were asked by Maa Myramayi in English, such as: "Guruji, what is happiness—ananda; what is the meaning of life; what are we all looking for..." and many more. This lasted for twenty minutes and I am not sure how many understood what she was saying. It was just like her Torah classes, about which my husband had told me. But Guruji translated the questions and answered them in English and Hindi.

'This was followed by bhajan-singing with harmonium and tabla for another ten minutes. By then, the fruit and milk were ready. Myra came into the kitchen with some women, took them and served them to the satsangis, making the first offering to Guruji. She had kept aside a silver plate and an ornate glass for him. The rest had disposable paper plates and cups.

'Myra did not ask me to join them. Maybe she was uncomfortable about me being in the holy presence of the guru.

'I did not understand her behaviour till much later. Even though I was angry, I put away the things, filled garbage bags and washed up. I was hurt and in tears, but wiped my eyes and spitefully picked up the curtain and hung it on the side of the door, so that I could have a good view of what was happening in the drawing room.

'The guru kept sitting as the satsangis started leaving after touching his feet. He blessed them as they bent over his "lotus feet". I had my eyes glued to the dais, as I did not want to miss seeing Maa Myramayi falling at the guru's feet. Some of the satsangis lay flat on the floor for his blessings. I wondered what Myra would do.

'But in the blink of an eye, I missed the scene as I bent to pick up a garbage bag. When I turned around, the house was empty. All I could see was the open front door, the colours of the rangoli and the flickering lights of the lamps. Disappointed, I assumed that Myra had gone downstairs with the guru.

'An hour later, I was still waiting in Myra's house, writing the accounts. Suddenly, I felt there was something amiss. I went to the balcony and called out to the security guard and asked him about the "gori" lady. He said that she was not downstairs, nor had he seen her leave in the guru's Mercedes. Maybe it was Guruji's "maya" that they had all disappeared in a split second. I peeped into her bedroom. It was stripped of all her personal belongings. Her backpack was missing. There was nothing there but the stuff we had bought, rented or borrowed. Just a single apple sitting happily on the dining-room table. Maybe it was symbolic. I am not intelligent enough to understand these matters; maybe Ruby could enlighten us about them. Daniyal had told me to charge her properly, as America is often known as the Big Apple. But I got nothing from the deal, neither big apple nor small. It dawned on me that Myra had cleared out and flown off unnoticed in the guru's chariot.

'The next best thing I could do was to send for Ezra. It was his bright idea to invite single young women to stay at Shalom India Housing Society. Myra had not been interested in any of our nice young men and nobody ever understood a word of her Torah lessons.

'I was always suspicious of Ezra's intentions when he drove Myra back and forth from the synagogue. Imagine, such a busy man had time for her! Good he stopped all that nonsense. I had half a mind to warn Sigaut about his interest in Myra. Now the bird has flown and how...'

✡

When Salome called Ezra from the security guard's intercom at the gate, he rushed down in his pyjamas. He was stupefied that Myra had left without a word of farewell. She had been his responsibility so he had to inform the police. What a mess!

The police carried out an investigation, but there was no trace of Myra. Nor had she taken a flight back to America. The police closed the file with a note, which stated, 'Disappeared into India.'

That night, as Salome helped Ezra switch off the lights and close Juliet's apartment, A-107, a holy number according to Maa Myramayi, she felt that Prophet Elijah was smiling down at Ezra mischievously.

3
Ruby

At a Hanukkah party at Shalom India Housing Society, Ruby was conscious of Lebana of Apartment A-110 watching her. Her look was a little too amorous for Ruby's comfort. Even while her husband Gershom was alive she was used to attention from men, but not women. It annoyed her.

It had been a pleasant evening but Lebana disturbed her. She was feeling a little dizzy when Lebana's niece Yael offered her a plate of food. She thanked her and sat down with the teenagers of the society. They wanted her to start a music class in the community hall of Shalom India Housing Society. Smiling graciously, she left her plate on an empty chair, refused the offer and went towards the Hanukkah tree installed between Block A and B. She was fond of Yael, as Yael resembled her married daughter who lived in Canada, so she had packed a small bottle of perfume in a shimmering cloth bag with Yael's name inscribed on it. She left it in a basket near the tree and turned around only to find herself face to face with Lebana.

As Lebana congratulated her for looking so elegant, her eyes drilled holes into Ruby's cleavage.

Ruby smirked. Lebana looked drab, like a 1950s Hindi film star, in an outdated lemon-yellow salwar kameez suit with violet sprays and an embroidered smock, worn with a net dupatta. She tried to smile as Lebana complimented her on her sari, her string of pearls and the colour of her lipstick. But her jaw dropped as the other woman closed her eyes, took a deep breath and asked, 'Which perfume are you wearing, Lily of the Valley?'

Ruby felt even more uncomfortable. She patted her hair, smiled and said, 'No, this is just an ordinary eau de toilette.'

'Ah! You speak French?' said Lebana. 'When I was in school, I studied French as a second language. I was good at languages. In fact, I always dreamt of going to Paris. Beautiful city. I saw it on a travel show on television. Have you been there? I cannot travel. Family responsibilities, you know…'

Ruby saw that her eyes were wet as she glanced at her widowed sister Abigail and Abigail's daughter Yael.

Lebana did not seem to notice that Ruby was being brusque when she said, 'No, I have not been to Paris. Yes, once when Gershom was alive, we had a stopover there … you know my daughter lives in Canada.'

'Did you see the Eiffel Tower?' Lebana leant towards Ruby, her eyes sparkling with excitement.

'No.'

Lebana persisted. 'And your daughter, does she speak French?'

Ruby shook her head and touched her temples. Lebana was giving her a headache.

Lebana immediately swung into action. Asking Ruby if she had a headache, she forced her to sit down, stood behind her and lightly massaged the back of her neck.

To Ruby's embarrassment, all eyes turned to them.

Ruby stood up, saying, 'I am fine, just a little tired.'

It was then that Lebana said something, which often came back to Ruby like a warning. She held Ruby's hands, looked deep into her eyes and said, 'You know, I am a trained nurse and can give you a very good massage. In the hospital where I worked, I was known for curing migraines. So, whenever you have a headache, call me…'

Aghast, Ruby noticed that while Lebana was talking about the massage, her hands were moving sensuously in the air, as though they were touching her body. She shivered, wondering if Lebana was a lesbian. She had heard about them, but never met one.

Ruby wondered if Abigail and Lebana…?

Her suspicions grew stronger when, a few months later, Abigail suddenly fell sick. She had high fever, nightmares and delirium. She kept thinking that a two-headed scorpion was attacking her. Night after night, she would wake up screaming and only calm down after Lebana gave her a sedative.

It was then that Lebana remembered that Ruby sometimes divined dreams and phoned her. 'For the last few nights, my sister Abigail has been having frightening dreams. I know you analyse dreams. Can you please help us?'

Ruby knew the limits of her powers and refused. 'I am sorry for Abigail, but it is better if you consult a doctor.'

'I have already taken her for a check-up and the doctor says there is nothing wrong. It could be menopause. But we both feel that if you interpret the dream, it would be of great help.'

Ruby softened when she heard Lebana crying at the other end of the line.

'Lebana, I really cannot help.'

Between sobs, Lebana said, 'I am so frightened and will feel better if you help Abigail.'

To dissuade her, Ruby asked, 'Have you checked for malaria? Sometimes, one gets such symptoms in malaria.'

'Dr Gonzales from Block-B came this morning and we asked the laboratory down the street to collect her blood samples. The reports are normal. Maybe there is more to her delirium.' Lebana lowered her voice. 'This is the month when Abigail had lost her husband.'

Ruby said, 'I am not a doctor, but if you insist, I will come.'

Lebana sounded relieved. 'Thank you. When will you come?'

'I can come today, at 3.30 in the afternoon.'

After playing the piano for an hour, Ruby meditated in her chair, ate a light lunch, had a short nap, woke up, dressed in a white pantsuit, brushed her hair, wore pale pink lipstick, dabbed a little perfume behind her ears, rang for the lift and braced herself to meet Lebana, hoping that she would not make any further obscene gestures.

When Ruby rang the bell of Lebana's apartment, she could feel another headache beginning. A maid opened the door and led her to Abigail's bedroom. The door was ajar and Ruby saw that Abigail was sleeping with a cold compress on her head. Lebana was reclining next to her, one hand on her head, the other on her stomach. Ruby had half a mind to turn back when the maid called out to Lebana.

Lebana jumped out of bed, apologizing. 'Sorry, we had a sleepless night and were resting.'

Ruby tried to ease the tension by asking, 'Where is Yael?'

Abigail's face suddenly lit up. 'Tuition,' she whispered. 'After the dream, she slept all night on my right and Lebana on my left. I was so frightened.'

Ruby was unsure of how to handle the situation. She had built up a reputation of divining dreams by reading some books. She cursed Salome under her breath for passing the word around that she had mystical powers. After Gershom's death, when she started interpreting dreams, her main intention was to pass time by meeting people without giving the impression that she was lonely.

To escape from Lebana, Ruby explained, 'I know very little about the meaning of dreams and am not a hundred per cent correct. I could not predict my own husband's death.' Saying this, she pulled out her lace-trimmed handkerchief, wiped her eyes and stood up to leave.

But she had misjudged Lebana's perseverance. 'We trust you,' Lebana said, rubbing her sister's soles, while the maid offered Ruby a glass of lemon juice.

Ruby smiled self-consciously and asked Abigail the details of the nightmare. Eyes closed, she listened, trying to understand the meaning of the dream.

Abigail said, 'As a rule, we go to bed early and wake up early. When I return from work, we lock up the house by 7, change into our nightclothes, have dinner and then we all go to bed. But when there is an event at the synagogue, we leave the apartment by 6.30 and return before 10.

'On Saturday afternoon and Sunday night, we watch something on TV. Sometimes Yael watches a film—she is crazy about The Mummy film series about Egypt. In fact, she brings home books on Egypt from the British Council Library. She also watches everything about Egypt on Discovery and National Geographic. Truthfully, Ruby, I do not like these films.' Lebana smiled indulgently as Abigail continued, 'Actually I like nothing better than a feel-good Hindi film. The other night, I went to bed at our usual time but around midnight, I woke up screaming when I had this dream...'

Ruby saw that Lebana's hands were moving over Abigail's head with the same sensuous movements as when she had offered her a massage on Hanukkah night.

Abigail looked helpless lying in Lebana's arms, her head resting on her sister's shoulder. She continued with her story, 'Last night,

Lebana told me that I was screaming in my sleep. I have never said this, but when Yael's father died, I had a similar dream. I dreamt that I was running in a dark lane and a shapeless creature was chasing me. I kept running and screaming. I could see myself running till I realized that the street was a dead end. I stood with my back pressed against the wall as this enormous black, inky creature raced towards me with a funny gait. It was a two-headed scorpion, its two tail-stings raised like flags over its head, its double pincers opening and closing like a pair of scissors about to chop off my head. I had a similar dream last night.'

Abigail sat up and lent against the pillow, perspiring profusely. Tears running down her cheeks, she asked Ruby, 'Do you think this is a bad omen?'

Ruby touched Abigail's cold hands as she tried to gain time to choose her words. She moved uncomfortably in her chair, stood up, went to the window and looked out. Franco Fernandez, an ageing Christian musician who lived in Block-B, was walking his dog in the garden below. Flushed and nervous, Ruby returned to her chair as Abigail said, 'I forgot to tell you that when I fell asleep again after Lebana gave me a sedative, the dream continued and I saw myself running under the scorpion's legs.'

Ruby smiled. 'Oh! That means the worst is over. You escaped the scorpion's pincers! It ran over you and disappeared. I see no danger. Believe me, tonight you will sleep well.'

Abigail looked relieved, smiled and thanked Ruby.

At the door, Lebana hugged Ruby and kissed her. Taken aback, Ruby leaned backwards, walked away, pressed the buzzer for the lift and quickly stepped into it. She was angry with herself for not slapping Lebana. She hated scenes and nobody at Shalom India Housing Society would understand why she had slapped mousy little Lebana. As the lift descended, she heard Lebana calling out,

'The perfume you gave Yael on Hanukkah was very good; I wear it every day...'

As the lift stopped at Ruby's floor, she made a mental note to stay away from the kiss of the scorpion woman.

4
Ruby and Georgie

Ruby switched off the DVD player, which had been playing Chaim Topol's *Fiddler on the Roof*. It was her favourite film and once a month, whenever she felt lonely, she would watch it and, to get back her good mood, play the theme song on her piano. But just as she opened the piano lid, the doorbell rang. Cautious by nature, she looked through the peephole. A stranger was standing there. She called out, 'Who is it...?'

He answered, 'Georgie, your old friend.'

She opened the door and looked at him. She did not think she knew him. Maybe her eyes were playing tricks on her or her cataract was getting worse: the man at the door looked strangely like Topol in the film. He was a tall, sturdy man with a bristly beard and was wearing a lopsided beret, just like Topol. The only difference was that instead of crumpled overalls, he was wearing an open-necked red shirt, showing off his rough chest hair. His big, broad smile was also like the film hero's.

The stranger laughed when he saw the suspicion in her eyes. As she was about to slam the door on his face, he held on to it, saying, 'Ruby, look, it's me, Georgie.'

It was then that her eyes fell on his beautiful, tapering musician's fingers and she let him in, saying, 'Sorry, I didn't recognize you.'

Georgie smiled, removed his beret, threw it on the carpet, bowed and said, 'Oh, my beautiful Ruby! How can you forget King George, your childhood sweetheart?'

Ruby burst out laughing. He stood in front of her with his lopsided smile brightening his face. She led him to the sofa chair and settled down in her straight-backed one. She remembered Georgie as a young man of eighteen but naturally, after so many years, he looked as old and scruffy as Topol, the patriarch in the film. Maybe he too was a father of five daughters.

As they chatted, the years seemed to slip away and Ruby felt as if she was falling in love with him all over again. He noticed her smile and teased, 'Look, isn't it amazing that after all these years, we are still in love…'

Ruby stiffened. In an effort to hide her feelings, she bent down, picked up his beret, put it on the table—she hated clutter—and went into the kitchen to get him a glass of water. He took the glass, brushing against her hand, looked at her, and asked, 'You and me…?'

'Come on, Georgie, no way … but good to see you after ages.'

Uncomfortable with his amorous gaze, Ruby tried to change the subject, asking, 'You are in Ahmedabad…?'

Georgie made himself comfortable, swung a leg over the hand rest, looked at her indulgently and asked for a cup of tea. 'Chai,' he said loudly, 'not your style of insipid Victorian British tea, but real tea, maybe with cardamom.'

Ruby stood up, patted her hair in place, looked down at him and said with a snigger, 'You haven't changed a bit, even after living in

America. You haven't forgotten your Gujarati habits. The maid has left for the day and I am not brewing that local stuff for you. It's my teatime and I will only make my type of tea.'

Georgie stood up suddenly with such agility that Ruby could not help admiring him. 'For your age you are really fit.'

Georgie puffed out his chest, tapped his fist on his bicep and said, 'That is because my heart is still young.' Then he followed her into the kitchen, and asked, 'Sweetheart, can I please make my own tea?'

Ruby gave him a strict look, saying, 'Well, if I remember correctly, you were brought up like a good Jewish boy, but now you look like a tramp. Sure, you can make your own desi tea.'

They made tea together, carried it out on a tray and laid it on the dining table. Hers was brewed lightly in a preheated white porcelain teapot with sprigs of violets. She had it lukewarm, with a teaspoon of cold milk and no sugar. His was made with cardamom, which he had found on her kitchen shelf, and double boiled with large quantities of milk and sugar. Ruby opened a box of macarons for him, which he refused, asking, 'Don't you have something salty?'

She raised her eyebrows, and asked, 'You mean Gujarati deep-fried snacks? Then you have knocked at the wrong door.'

Georgie raised his cup and asked, 'Is that why you married Gershom? Good, square, dependable.'

'You have a short memory. Before my parents could give an answer to the proposal sent by yours, you had left for America.'

'That's not entirely true. You knew I was waiting for you.'

'Not really, for in a year we were told you had married an American girl, while I was still unmarried and working as a secretary. That was when Gershom, just returned from London, saw me at the synagogue in Mumbai and sent a proposal. I liked his neat, nice, distinguished looks and agreed…'

'You mean I was shabby, dirty and not good enough for you.'

'Well, you didn't have Gershom's class.'

'Sure, how boring…'

Ruby's hand, which sported a diamond wedding ring, trembled. 'You are mean. How can you talk like that about my late husband?'

'Sorry, Ruby, I didn't mean to hurt you. I met both of you a year after you were married and except for the fact that he was mild-mannered, well-dressed and neat, as you said, I noticed he could pour whisky with style. And that was it. I assume you must have yawned through the years you were together. '

Ruby placed her cup on the table carefully, stood up and, pointing to the door, ordered Georgie to get out of her house, as she still respected her husband. Georgie sat frozen in the chair, then burst out laughing. 'It was a joke,' he said and falling on his knees, begged her forgiveness with folded hands.

He noticed Ruby's face crumbling and although she stood in front of him like an army general, tears flowed down her cheeks. Astounded, Georgie stood up and sheepishly held her hands. To his surprise, she fell into his arms, whispering, 'Georgie, why did you go away?' He held her gently and kissed her passionately.

She led him to her bedroom. After a moment's indecision, they made love awkwardly. Later, bathed and dressed, they avoided looking at each other, so Georgie suggested that they cook, something quick and simple. He said that they could make pasta in a cheese sauce. They ate from the same plate, sometimes feeding each other, and laughed over Georgie's anecdotes about his first few years in America. Then he told her that he had separated from his wife Victoria and had been living in Auroville, Puducherry, for the last two years where he was a ceramist working in an American friend's studio. Ruby was impressed that he had made a name for himself in the world of pottery. Before leaving, he opened his shoulder bag, pulled out a brown paper packet and handed it to her. To her delight, it was a coffee mug with a warm blue glaze. They kissed and with a heavy heart, Ruby let Georgie return to his hotel room.

Georgie stayed in Ahmedabad for a week and they spent a euphoric seven days cooking, eating and making love. He would arrive every day at noon. Ruby cancelled all her appointments and asked her maid to come early in the morning, telling her that she was holding a music workshop in a school. Whenever her neighbours in Shalom India Housing Society asked her whether she had a guest, as they often saw Georgie going up to her apartment, she said that he was a distant cousin, who had been living in America and had returned after some forty years. He was in Ahmedabad on business, had traced her and they were catching up on old times. But if someone such as Salome wanted to know his family lineage, as she knew most Bene Israel Jews, Ruby snubbed her, saying that she had no idea about his village name, which would indicate his origins. Ruby was annoyed when Sippora, who was from Mumbai, saw Georgie at Ruby's door and stopped to speak to him. 'I think you are a Bombay Jew. I have a feeling we have met...'

That was when Ruby interrupted with a tight smile and said, 'Let me introduce John, Gershom's best friend when they were studying in London. He has come to see me.' As Georgie entered her apartment, she did not invite Sippora to join them and quickly closed the door, almost on Sippora's face. Annoyed by her behaviour, Georgie wanted to know why she had been impolite to her neighbour. Ruby told him that she could not take the risk of a scandal at Shalom India Housing Society. They respected her and she did not want to give the impression that she was a merry widow. He shrugged, saying, 'I don't understand you. Maybe someone will recognize me, as I belong to a well-known Jewish family of Mumbai. How long can you hide our affair? Maybe we will get married eventually.'

Ruby folded her arms, saying, 'When it comes to that, we will see how to announce our wedding. It will not be easy, but leave it to me.'

Georgie was restless and, much to Ruby's annoyance, left early without a hug or kiss. She was in tears and even though she tried, she could not stop him. She spent the day playing the piano and waiting for him to return. When he did not, she called him on his cell phone late in the evening. She was relieved when he answered cheerfully and told her that he was on his way to her place. They would have a candlelight dinner.

Ruby dressed in a short black skirt and a sleeveless silver-spangled blouse she had not worn in years, along with a diamond choker and heart-shaped diamond earrings. She painted her lips a bright red, dabbed perfume in her cleavage and slipped on a pair of red heels. When she opened the door, Georgie was standing there with his usual lopsided grin and beret falling over his left eye. He was carrying bags of food he had bought from the Old City— kebabs, tandoori chicken, samosas and roomali rotis. He told her what a great time he had had roaming the streets of Ahmedabad. He was famished.

She took one look at the packets of food and crinkled her nose. 'This is unhygienic.'

He did not answer, went for a shower and asked her to heat the food. He also asked her to light a candle for Sabbath. Ruby was touched and set the table. Then they stood together and said the Sabbath prayers. Georgie ate all that he had bought while watching Ruby pick at a bowl of salad.

After his return to Puducherry, Georgie called Ruby almost every day, often late at night, disturbing her sleep. They talked and giggled, exchanging sweet nothings like teenagers.

Ruby's secret life continued for a year until Christmas, when Georgie proposed to her. On the last day of Hanukkah, he said,

'This is my Hanukkah gift to you. Since my divorce, in fact much before it, I have been very lonely. I am sure you are also lonely since Gershom died. Now that we have met, let us start a new life. Since you are so worried about comments from our community, we could settle in America. I still have an apartment in California. We could get married soon and leave for America. You can keep your apartment in Ahmedabad and once we are married, people will accept us and we can live between both countries. I am sure you can convince your daughter to accept me. I will wait for your answer…'

The unexpected proposal frightened her. She pleaded for time. She had enjoyed the time they had spent together, but feared treading unknown terrain. Suddenly, she felt she did not know him.

Ruby asked Georgie for a week. Every day she sat at her piano, wondering if she was willing to give up the comfort and predictability of her life at A-104, Shalom India Housing Society.

That was when Ruby had another guest—cousin Irene from America. Irene was related to Georgie and her arrival was a godsend for Ruby. She was to stay for a week—almost the same amount of time that Ruby had asked for to tell Georgie her final decision.

Irene wanted to try Indian street food, which she missed in America. They spent long hours eating and shopping. Ruby did not know how to ask her about Georgie, as she did not want to tell Irene that she was in love with him.

Then one evening, Ruby ordered a special Bene Isaeli dinner made by Elisheba, wife of Cantor Saul Ezekiel and the community caterer, for Irene. Irene was pleased to see the green masala fish curry and, while passing the rice and chapattis to her, Ruby asked her casually if she had met Georgie in California.

Irene's hand froze in mid-air. She looked suspiciously at Ruby. 'How come after all these years you are asking me about Georgie? I remember you were to be married, but he disappeared and you married Gershom. Must say, a much better choice than Georgie.

Have you met him recently? I know he is in Puducherry. Did the lecher come here?'

'Not really.'

'What do you mean, "not really"?'

'Well, I saw him.'

'Where …'

'Right here …'

'When?'

'Last month.'

'Well …'

'Did you meet him often in California?'

'Of course …'

'What does he do there?'

'Why?'

'Because in Puducherry he is a potter …'

'Oh yeah …'

Irene's eyes blazed. 'Ruby, you are hiding something from me.'

Ruby's eyes brimmed with tears. 'Irene, I don't know what to do. I am in love with Georgie.'

'So what next?'

'I want to marry him. I have been so lonely.'

'Marry Georgie?'

'Yes.'

'Are you mad?'

'I don't know what to do. He was here for a week.'

'I am sure he used all his charm on you.'

'I can't explain. I felt like I was sixteen and in love all over again.'

'He plays the same game with all women.'

'What do you mean?'

'My husband Mordecai and I have kept in touch with Georgie since we all went to America together. We often met, as Georgie is my cousin. And, when he married Victoria, we had the reception at our place. They had met on a blind date. It was a whirlwind affair. Remember, he ditched you for Victoria—a real American blonde, just the type Indian men fantasize about.'

'I know, but he was so young...'

'Don't justify his actions just because he came and swept you off your feet, knowing that you were lonely since dear Gershom passed away.'

'In a way, I agree with you.'

'Let me tell you, Victoria was a wonderful wife to him. He behaved himself for the first three years, since she supported him. And, by the way, he has never done a jot of work his whole life.'

'But he told me he is doing well as a potter.'

'Lies ... when he married Victoria he knew she would support him, as she was in love with him. But she had not completed her studies. So she first worked as a cashier at a mall and went to school late in the evening. In two years, she had a diploma. She worked as a secretary in a law firm and, as he did not want to study, she found him a job as a waiter at a friend's restaurant. He was interested in art, so she sent him to art school. That was where he learnt pottery.'

'She must be a wonderful person.'

'Yes, she was committed to him and worked hard to make ends meet.'

'Then what went wrong?'

'Well, the same old story. He had an affair with his pottery teacher who was twice his age. Victoria told me that once she came home early and found them in her bed. She kicked them both out of the house.'

'Must have been awful for Victoria...'

'She was broken, and it took her a long time to get back to normal.'

'What happened to Georgie?'

'He was almost on the streets. But Mordecai took pity on him and put him up in our extra room. However, when his potter friend started visiting him at our place, I put my foot down and asked Georgie to leave. Soon after, his lady love ditched him. She was married with a family and did not want to change anything in her life. Anyway, she had no intention of settling down with him. But she need not have worried; women find him charming and he had a series of girlfriends. We continued to invite him for Sabbath dinner every Friday evening and knew all that was going on in his life. Then he introduced us to Myra, better known as Maa Myramayi. After that, his life seemed to change for the better.'

Ruby looked shell-shocked as she asked, 'Did I hear correctly, Myra ... Myramayi? Not the one who lived in Ahmedabad some time back, in Juliet's apartment?'

'I think so. She told us that she had lived in Ahmedabad for a year. I remember I asked her if she had met you, but she was not sure. She gave me some mumbo-jumbo about a Ruby who divines dreams. Do you?'

Ruby was embarrassed. 'No, she must have mixed me up with someone else.'

'She had gone to Rishikesh to an ashram with her guru but eventually returned to America and became part of some religious sect. Truthfully, I don't understand her at all.'

'So, she was Georgie's companion at that point.'

'No ... they have been together for many years.'

'Oh...'

'Didn't he tell you? She was in Ahmedabad and he had even asked her to meet you. The creep ... Myra is a kinky old woman ... looks much older than him ... she is also a potter. That is how he met her. And hold your breath! She is Georgie's live-in partner. They work together, live together and she has given him the freedom to live as he fancies, because she knows he will always return to her. She is his lover, sister, mother, all rolled in one.'

'He told me his friend in Puducherry was a man...'

'What else did he tell you?'

'He proposed marriage and said that we would live in America but I should keep this apartment so that we could live in both countries.'

'Ruby, you are really naive. Georgie will never marry you. He is still married to Victoria.'

'And Victoria?'

'She lives with Martin, a lawyer. They do not plan to get married.'

'How could he do this to me?'

'He can, because that's all he does.'

Ruby was in tears. 'Tell me, Irene, what should I do?'

'Forget him.'

That night, on Irene's insistence, Ruby called Georgie. A recorded message responded, 'This number does not exist.'

5

Yael

WHEN YAEL WAS in her early twenties, she decided that if she ever got married, she would choose a rich man. She was a computer engineer and doing well financially. She did not really need a husband to support her. Her mother Abigail and aunt Lebana had hinted that they were receiving many proposals for her. Quietly, Yael would listen to what they said about the suitors and their financial status. But whenever they asked her if she would consider a certain young man, she would refuse.

At the synagogue, where they had Sunday Hebrew classes, malidas, festivals, engagements, mehendis, weddings and other events, Yael had studied most of the bachelors of the community and rejected them. She was friendly with them and sometimes even flirted with them, but she knew that nobody could live up to her idea of a husband. Abigail and Lebana were worried that Yael might have a runaway marriage with a non-Jew one day and were anxious that she was so friendly with her immediate boss in the office. They took great pride in the fact that she was a well-brought-up Jewish girl. She was always back home by 6.30 p.m. She had told them that after office hours, other employees hung around at a café near the office, but she never joined them, though they teased her that she led a boring life and was tied to her mother's apron strings. After office, she would take a bus home and not stop at a mall, even when she wanted to buy a bottle of nail polish. Occasionally, when there was an office party, a colleague's birthday, wedding anniversary or farewell, she would take her mother's permission to stay late but make sure that someone from the office dropped her home by 9 p.m. She realized that if she came home late, both Abigail and Lebana would be waiting for her in the drawing room, watching a late-night movie on television, or on the balcony, watching the road leading to the main gate. She visualized their tense faces and decided that she would rather be home early and follow their strict timings as she had always done since she was a child.

Abigail and Lebana were proud of their beautiful Yael. Tall, slim and always dressed in full-sleeved kurtis over jeans with a dupatta, her shoulder-length hair in a ponytail or left open, she was the image of a good Jewish girl. Whenever she dressed up in an embroidered kurta and sequinned dupatta and wore make-up, it was for an event at the synagogue.

After all their efforts to get Yael married to a Bene Israel Jew from Ahmedabad failed, Abigail and Lebana spread the word through relatives in Mumbai, Thane and Israel that they were looking for a groom for her. Soon, they started receiving more marriage proposals. Yael checked out each one of them and told her mother and aunt that they should stop looking for prospective grooms, as she had studied the background of each prospect and was not interested in anyone.

One weekend, when her mother had a holiday from the school where she taught English, Yael surprised them by returning home early with a carton of cupcakes, made tea and said that she wanted to speak to them. Abigail and Lebana sat around their small dining table, assuming that she would tell them she was in love with her boss. They were relieved when Yael broached the subject of her marriage but did not mention her boss. She told them that the grooms they had suggested were not suitable. And even if the suitors from Israel looked promising, they were not for her. Abigail and Lebana tried to explain to Yael that money was not everything; finding a good Jewish husband was important.

Yael did not agree and said that she had decided to stay unmarried for the rest of her life. Defeated, mother and aunt accepted her decision, assuming that it was a temporary one to ward off their matchmaking. They hoped that she would change her mind when she found the right partner.

Soon, Abigail and Lebana stopped matchmaking. This lasted till Yael celebrated her thirtieth birthday. Secretly, they worried about her male colleagues, married or unmarried. Yael often invited her women friends for high tea and once a year, she would invite her entire office staff for dinner. At these parties, her friendliness with the men bothered her mother and aunt. Even more so when she had long conversations on her cell phone or sat for hours on the sofa, sending text messages.

Yael was becoming increasingly secretive, so both mother and aunt were sure that she would have a runaway marriage with a non-Jew. They often discussed Yael and wondered if she had a boyfriend, not necessarily from the office. Abigail would defend her daughter at such times, saying that she was friendly but never coquettish.

Then one day everything changed. It was at the Passover Seder organized by the synagogue, where there was an American family of six, a long-faced Jew from Venezuela with dreadlocks and a bespectacled South African Jew.

Usually, during a Passover ceremony, families sat together and Yael shared the table with her mother and aunt. But on that particular day, she came late from office to the synagogue and there was no place for her. So Ezra led her to the centre table he had set aside for their foreign guests and Yael found herself sitting between the Venezuelan and the South African. Both were young and Yael was uncomfortable, as she felt all eyes on her. After all, she was a young unmarried woman and people would assume that she was flirting with the two. Self-conscious, she almost stood up to leave when she noticed Ruby sitting at the head of the table. Ruby had noticed her discomfiture and gave her a reassuring smile. Seated between the two men, who smiled at her, Yael nodded with the hint of a smile. They introduced themselves. The Venezuelan's name was Arial and the South African was Yohan. Yael introduced herself, throwing nervous glances around her. Soon, they started talking and Yael relaxed. An Indian Passover Seder being different from those held in other countries, Yael explained the rites and rituals to them.

At some point during the conversation, she heard Yohan speak in Gujarati. He asked her whether he was supposed to drink the sherbet or just hold the glass in his hand. Yael smiled and answered in Gujarati. She was impressed. When there was a break in the prayers, she asked where he had learnt the language.

In an hour, Yael gathered a lot of information about Yohan. He had grown up in Johannesburg, South Africa, where his neighbours were Patels from Gujarat. Thanks to this family, he had developed a love for Gujarati food, language and lifestyle. Later, he had taken lessons in Gujarati, but by profession, he was a professor of sociology. He had met an Ahmedabad-based litterateur, Professor Makwana, at a conference in New York, who had spoken about Gujarati literature and recited a poem. Yohan was so impressed that he had followed him to Ahmedabad, after arrangements for Yohan's accommodation were made near the professor's home. Like all travelling Jews, he had wanted to attend the Passover Seder services at a synagogue. Professor Makwana knew Ezra and made arrangements for Yohan to be at the synagogue.

When Yohan started taking lessons from Professor Makwana, he had insisted that the young man should speak in Gujarati. So Yohan was happy to practise Gujarati with Yael, who complimented him on his almost-perfect accent. Yohan was pleased.

Abigail and Lebana were watching Yael from a distance and were uncomfortable with her sudden interest in the foreigner. He was friendly and by the end of the evening, Yael and he had exchanged phone numbers.

Much to Abigail and Lebana's surprise, after the Seder, Yael informed them that she had invited Yohan for tea over the weekend.

When Yohan arrived, Yael was late in coming from work. He stood in the doorway and charmed Abigail and Lebana by greeting them with a namaste. He looked handsome in a maroon khadi kurta worn over jeans. As they waited for Yael, he asked them questions about the Jewish community of Ahmedabad. They were impressed that he was a linguist and, besides Gujarati, could speak Hindi, Hebrew, French and Spanish. When Yael arrived, the older women left the young people alone and started preparations for tea, as Yohan had requested them to make Gujarati tea for him, with ginger and cardamom.

That night, Yael informed her mother that she would be giving Gujarati lessons to Yohan twice a week, and he would have Sabbath dinner with them. She was not asking permission but making a statement. Abigail and Yael accepted her decision, as they were happy that she was taking an interest in a young man. What did it matter that he was from South Africa? After all, he was Jewish and that was more important than anything else.

So on Wednesdays and Fridays, Yael came back home early and one thing led to another. Yael and Yohan started spending Sunday afternoons together. He became part of the family and almost always stayed on for dinner. They turned a deaf ear to rumours circulating in Shalom India Housing Society that Yael and Yohan were having an affair. To counter the gossip, Lebana informed everyone that Yohan had a girlfriend in America and asked, 'Have you ever seen Yael go out with Yohan? They do not even go to the café round the corner; they always meet when we are at home. They are just good friends.'

When the young men of Shalom India Housing Society teased Yohan about his American girlfriend, he smiled broadly and cracked jokes in Gujarati, which nobody understood but everybody laughed at.

Yohan was funny and friendly. He attended all festivals, malidas and community dinners at the society and also joined the early morning laughing club. Once in a while, he met Ruby and played the piano with her, which annoyed Yael. He also visited Franco Fernandez late at night, chatted with him and played his violin as Yael stood on her balcony, listening to him.

All rumours came to an end when Yael hosted a farewell dinner for Yohan. He was leaving India and going to New York and she wanted to introduce him to her office friends. Yael had made plum juice, vegetable biryani, salad and dal. Yohan had brought mango ice cream for everybody. The menu was planned by Yael and Yohan, who behaved like co-hosts of the party. Abigail and Lebana were suspicious and exchanged knowing glances.

A week after Yohan left, Abigail asked Yael if she had heard from him. She shook her head and said, 'I just received a thank-you card in my email.'

Soon, life returned to normal and the hope that Abigail had nurtured that Yael would marry Yohan was forgotten, although she had made a secret wish and asked Prophet Elijah to play matchmaker.

The Prophet answered her prayers through speed post. In six months, two days before the Jewish New Year, Yohan was back in

Ahmedabad, not to study Gujarati, but to ask for Yael's hand in marriage. His parents had flown down with him to see the bride-to-be and were staying at a hotel.

Unknown to Abigail and Lebana, Yael and Yohan had been communicating through Skype and had decided to get married.

Abigail and Lebana invited Yohan and his parents for dinner. As soon as Yael opened the door, Yohan knelt in the doorway, held Yael's hand in his and asked her to marry him. Yael accepted his proposal and they spent the evening having fun and laughing as Abigail and Lebana served the best of Bene Israel cuisine that they had asked Elisheba to cook for them. When dinner ended with the typical Bene Israel rose-coloured chik-cha-halwa, traditionally made for New Year, Yohan slipped a diamond ring on Yael's finger and they were declared engaged. Yohan kissed Yael, went to the balcony and made a loud and clear announcement to the residents of Shalom India Housing Society that he was in love with her. Ezra immediately held an impromptu party, ordered a big cake and celebrated the event on the society lawns. Everybody shook hands, wished the couple 'Mazal tov' to the tune of Franco Fernandez's violin and danced till late into the night.

As Yohan and his parents got ready to leave in their rented car, Lebana took Yohan aside and said, 'Do you mind if I ask you a personal question?'

'Anything you want to ask, Aunty.'

'I do not know much about your society, but I know marriages don't last there.' With tears in her eyes, she added, 'Promise me that you will never leave Yael...'

Yohan gave her a warm hug and in true Bollywood style said, '*Nahin, kabhi nahin*...never.'

6
Raphael

EVEN THOUGH RAPHAEL did not have an apartment at Shalom India Housing Society, nor is he a bride, he is part of this story. All the residents felt that he was part of their lives. Raphael often arrived like a pre-monsoon storm. His visits were sudden and when he came, he brought a certain joie de vivre with him.

Ezra and Raphael had gone to the same school and grown up playing cricket in the backyard of the synagogue. Ezra was very fond of Raphael and thought that Raphael was mischievous, but not malicious. Sometimes, his sudden arrival disturbed the still waters of Shalom India Housing Society.

The general gossip was that he came to Ahmedabad to meet Sippora. There seemed to be no other reason. It was an open secret that he had never gotten over his boyhood crush on her. Raphael seemed to be blind to the fact that he was the reason for the innumerable quarrels between Sippora and her husband Opher.

Only Ezra knew that Raphael kept returning to Ahmedabad for other reasons. He had to cope with his personal ghosts: the death of his parents and the disposal of his ancestral house on S.G. Road along with a dilapidated two-storeyed ancestral bungalow behind the synagogue. Both houses had numerous artifacts, books and furniture, which had to be sold or given away before he bid a final farewell to Ahmedabad. But even if he did so, there was one object that fettered him to the city of his birth—his mother's piano. He was sentimental about it and could neither sell it nor donate it to a school. Unused, it was like a coffin of memories and cast a long shadow over his life. It had become a symbol of death. Sippora was a pleasant distraction.

Some elders still remembered how, when Sippora had come to Ahmedabad as a young bride, Raphael had not made any bones about his attraction for the leggy beauty from Bombay. Shamelessly he would stare at her as she stood in the women's gallery upstairs in the synagogue. If his father Victor nudged him, whispering, 'Don't stare at her,' he would hiss back, 'At least I don't look at her secretly like the others.' His father would look around and see that the other men were sneaking glances at Sippora too. It was well known in Ahmedabad's tiny Jewish community that Raphael was the main reason for the first big quarrel between Sippora and Opher.

That evening, they were bidding for the right to open and close the doors of the Ark, where the Torahs were kept, which would give the victorious bidder the right to carry them. Opher won and was carrying the biggest Torah, as he wanted to impress Sippora. Raphael was part of the group of men, dancing shoulder to shoulder with Opher. It was then that Raphael looked up at the women's gallery and saw Sippora standing next to the marble plaque of the Ten Commandments, where it was clearly written in Hebrew and Marathi—'Thou shall not covet thy neighbour's wife'. Sippora was wearing a red sheath dress with a slit at the knee, which exposed a long, shapely leg. She was leaning over the railing and watching her husband, her body moving rhythmically to the chants of Simha-Torah, when she noticed Raphael dancing with abandon. She smiled at him appreciatively. Pleased, Raphael laughed and waved at her. That very moment, Opher looked up to see if Sippora was watching him and was happy that she was waving in his direction. But pleasure turned to anger when Opher realized that Sippora was waving at Raphael. With the Torah in his arms, Opher was helpless. All he could do was to look up at his wife with a severe expression, hoping she would understand that he did not approve of such brazen behaviour. He was sure that the other women in the congregation were laughing at her for waving at Raphael, even though he was just a teenager. Sippora saw his stern look, but ignored it.

Opher and Sippora returned home in stony silence. Later, they had their first fight. Opher alleged that Sippora had been flirting with Raphael. Sippora laughed at the idea, saying that Raphael was only a child. Opher exploded and Sippora walked out of the house. There were many rumours as to where she had spent the night. Had she gone to meet Raphael or had she checked into a hotel? All night long Opher kept calling up her friends till he fell asleep on the sofa. In his wildest dreams he had not imagined that Sippora was right there at Shalom India Housing Society, downstairs in Salome's house. Next morning, Salome sent her back.

Sippora tiptoed into the kitchen, made a cup of tea for Opher and woke him up with a kiss. If anyone thought that the quarrels would end with the years, they did not. Sippora and Opher fought regularly over trivial issues but stuck together, as they loved each other. And, through the years, they continued to fight over Raphael even after they had had children.

✡

Raphael had grown up in Ahmedabad, but since the age of seventeen, he had been living in Singapore with his uncle. His father Victor was a well-known doctor in Ahmedabad and his mother Daisy was a music teacher. Raphael was born to Daisy late in life, when she was way into her forties. After a series of tests, the doctors had declared that Victor and Daisy could not have a child. But Daisy was undaunted and gave the example of the matriarch Sarah, who had conceived late in life. She took the blessings of both Hindu and Muslim saints. Victor, who did not believe in this sort of voodoo, prayed to Prophet Elijah to bless them with a child. Later that year, on a beautiful full-moon night, Victor was sitting in the balcony, reading a novel, and felt like having a drink. He went to the drawing-room cabinet, poured himself a peg of whisky, switched off the lights and returned to the balcony. It was then that he experienced a strange aura and felt the Prophet's presence in their house. Except for the reading lamp next to his chair, the house was dark, but he noticed that the picture of Prophet Elijah was illuminated. Feeling blessed, he settled down in the balcony and continued reading. But he could not concentrate on the words. He was thinking of Daisy and wondering if she could get pregnant at forty-plus. If she did, that would be a miracle. Then, realizing the futility of his dreams, he sighed, switched off the lights, went into the bedroom, lay down next to Daisy and took her in his arms. Eyes closed, she smiled. A couple of months later, Daisy went for her regular check-up and could not believe her ears when the gynaecologist congratulated her, saying that she was pregnant.

That year Raphael was born. He often recounted this story to Sippora, adding that perhaps his father had read the *Kamasutra* that night. Raphael never told anyone, including Sippora, that she reminded him of his mother.

When Daisy was alive, she would play the piano for her son or they would play records on the old gramophone. One of Raphael's most treasured memories was when she taught him to waltz. His idyllic childhood came to an end when Victor realized that his son was not interested in studies. There were regular arguments between father and son. Often Daisy intervened, but could not establish peace between them. Being musically inclined, she understood why Raphael was not interested in his studies, but for Victor, it was sacrilege that the young man was wasting his time listening to music and playing the piano. So, though Raphael had not finished his schooling, Victor sent him to Singapore. Daisy was heartbroken, but Victor insisted on this because he was sure that his brother Jonah, a schoolteacher, would instil some regard for education in the young man.

When Raphael left for Singapore, Daisy went into depression and Victor lost all interest in life. Within a year, Victor was unable to handle Daisy's long silences. He realized he had made a mistake in separating mother and son. He was doubly upset when Jonah informed him that Raphael had become a school dropout, left home and only returned to Jonah when he needed money.

So Victor asked Raphael to return to India. Back home, he would be under his mother's eye and she would be happy. Maybe she could even persuade him to go back to school. He had just one more year to finish school and Victor even suggested that he study music. Later, they could buy him a good music system and help him set up a business of renting out sound systems. It was big business in Ahmedabad and there was no denying that Raphael had an ear for music. But after Raphael joined a small rock band, he refused to return. His parents' pleas and threats fell on deaf ears.

For months, there was no news of him. A year later, Jonah called Victor and told him that Raphael had been traced to the address of Nataly, a twenty-something curvaceous blonde, the lead singer of his band. Another year passed. When Jonah informed Raphael about his mother's depression, he was concerned and immediately returned to India. Jonah warned Victor not to expect anything from the visit, as Raphael had changed. Victor did not know how to break the news to Daisy and decided to let things take their course.

A new drama unfolded when Raphael returned to Ahmedabad. Early that morning, when the doorbell rang, Daisy opened the door, assuming it was the milkman. Victor would remember the scene till his dying day. Daisy did not recognize her son, as he was dressed in bizarre cowboy clothes; his hair was dyed red, he was wearing bracelets and had an untidy stubble on his chin. He was not alone. Behind him, she saw the spiked heads of two girls and another scruffy young man with a long beard and dreadlocks. When Raphael tried to hug her, Daisy banged the door shut on his face, called out to Victor and screamed, 'Call the police.'

Victor opened the door, but did not hug his son. He shook hands formally and invited the group into the house. Daisy watched them from a distance as they heaved their backpacks on to her neat sofas covered with delicate lace. Suddenly, her mood changed from fear to anger. She rushed towards Raphael, held him by the elbow and shouted angrily, 'Don't you dare insult me by entering my house dressed like a loafer.' She dragged him to the door and threw him out, followed by his friends, then shut the door on their faces.

Victor tried to intervene, but Daisy would have none of it and stood with her back to the door, not allowing her husband to open it. A broken-hearted Raphael took the next flight to Mumbai and returned to Singapore within a week. Before leaving he spoke to his father, asking him to tell his mother that he was sorry. All Victor could manage was, 'God bless you.'

Raphael never saw his mother again, but started doing well as a pianist. To keep in touch with his parents, he regularly sent them cassettes of his music and greeting cards for the Jewish New Year. He pleased Uncle Jonah by landing up at his house on the first day of Passover dressed in a suit. He also accompanied Jonah to the synagogue for Yom Kippur prayers, fasting for a day and repenting for having caused so much pain to his mother. Raphael was sure that Uncle Jonah would inform his parents that he cared for them.

Gradually, Raphael heard of signs of thawing in his mother. Jonah told him that Daisy had displayed Raphael's photographs on the mantelpiece. Whenever friends, relatives or neighbours would drop in, she would speak about her son with pride, telling them that he had made a name for himself as a pianist. And, when she was in a good mood, she would play Raphael's cassettes, beating the tune on her knee and telling her guests that the music was a trifle loud, but her son had a good ear for music.

Encouraged, Raphael decided to make another trip to India. It was two years since he had seen his mother. But before he could fix a date, his father called him early one morning, saying that his mother had had a cardiac arrest and died in her sleep.

Raphael took the next flight home to bury Daisy. He was inconsolable when he returned from the graveyard. He realized that he would never see his mother again. He wanted to tell her that although she thought he was morally wrong in terms of his dress and conduct, he was happy in the life he had chosen. He had wanted her to accept him the way he was. He owed everything to her. It was she who had exposed him to the beautiful world of music and encouraged him to be creative. But when he tried to lead his own life, she could not accept it. So, after her death, year after year, he would fast on the Day of Atonement, hoping that she would forgive him.

On the night of Daisy's funeral, when the last mourner had left, Victor had broken down. They had been life partners and not been separated even for a day. When Victor switched off the light, he did not have the heart to enter their bedroom, so instead he slept on the sofa in the drawing room. Raphael sat at the piano, playing his mother's favourite tunes. It was then that he heard his father crying.

He turned around. Victor was sprawled out on the sofa, weeping like a child. Raphael cradled his father in his arms as tears flowed down his cheeks. Victor held on to him and made him promise that he would return to bury his father. Raphael promised, saying that he would always be there for him. He gave Victor a stiff brandy, led him to his own bedroom, tucked him into a quilt and lay next to him till he fell asleep. Later, he went to his mother's bed and slipped under the cover, feeling the warmth of her body, which had lain there only a few hours earlier. Clutching the bedclothes, he cried like a baby, hoping she would suddenly appear and hold him in her arms.

To make up for lost time, Raphael now often returned to India with Nataly, as Victor had taken a liking to her. His formerly disapproving father had accepted him the way he was. But whenever Nataly was in Ahmedabad, Victor made sure that nobody in the Jewish community knew about her. He maintained the pretence that his son was still the most eligible bachelor in town. Raphael and Nataly followed the rules and did not give Victor any reason to worry. In fact, they were happy to be together, listening to music, travelling around Gujarat or even helping Nataly wear a sari with the help of their driver Rodriques' wife, Maria.

Their utopia ended five years later when Victor got prostate cancer. Raphael locked up the house and took his father to Singapore. Within a year, Victor knew the disease had spread and wanted to return home to Ahmedabad. Raphael returned with him and made arrangements for him with Rodriques and Maria, who stayed in the outhouse of their bungalow.

When Victor's condition worsened, Raphael could not fly back to India. His father died in hospital. Ezra called Raphael and gave him the news. At the time Raphael was in the midst of a concert in Rome, so all he could do was to request Ezra to bury his father.

It was a difficult year for Raphael. He was booked for shows all over Europe and could not travel to India. To add to his problems,

Nataly became pregnant that year and although they continued with their concerts, she was always sick and in bad humour. It was the beginning of innumerable arguments between them. They were not married and Raphael suddenly had doubts about bringing a child born out of wedlock into the world. He believed that the child needed a name and family. But Nataly refused to get married. During this confusing time, Raphael needed his mother more than ever, as she would have found a solution to his problems. Moreover, he was weighed down with the rituals after his father's death. Ezra called him twice a month, insisting that he return to perform the one-year ceremony for his father. Raphael was distressed and Nataly could not sympathize with his problems. Finally, he found a pianist to replace him and flew to India. Torn between his father's grave and his unborn child, Raphael chose to bury the dead.

Back in Ahmedabad, much against Ezra's advice, Raphael stayed in his father's house on S.G. Road. Rodriques and Maria looked after all of his needs. This arrangement worked for him. He needed to unwind in his own home, although he found it hard to sleep in an empty house. Nataly often called at midnight, but they always ended up arguing over small things. Then, soon afterwards, Nataly lost their baby and broke up with Raphael at a time when he needed her the most.

The night after the one-year ceremony, when the last mourner had left, Raphael closed the door, gave Rodriques the day off and was sitting at the piano when the doorbell rang. It was Sippora. They shook hands. She offered her condolences and noticed that his face was wet with tears. Instinctively, she took him in her arms. They stood there holding each other as Raphael told her about his father and the baby he had lost.

Sippora wiped his tears and caressed his head. But she was suddenly uncomfortable when she felt his hands move over her breasts. His eyes were closed, the tears were still flowing and Sippora knew that at that moment, he just needed to be with another human being. She held him as though he was her child, although she knew that later she would regret her actions. But she was frightened when she heard Raphael call out to Daisy, saying, 'Mama, take me with you, don't leave me alone…' She gently pushed him away, took his hands in hers, helped him sit down and left.

Thereafter, whenever Raphael returned to India and met Sippora, he did not flirt with her, nor did he mention the incident. So much so that Sippora was not even sure whether Raphael remembered what had happened that night. But she made sure that they never met alone.

Raphael mourned his father's death for many years. He did not settle down with any of his innumerable girlfriends. He liked to joke with Sippora about his single status, saying that he had not yet found the woman who possessed his rib. God must have created a woman for him from his rib, but she was lost somewhere in the universe.

After a few years, he sold his house to Rodriques for a pittance and donated his mother's piano to the community hall of Shalom India Housing Society. This inspired Ruby to start a music class. He stopped coming to Ahmedabad after that.

When Raphael eventually disappeared, everybody felt it was for the common good, as Sippora and Opher could now live happily ever after. There were rumours that he had become a well-known pianist. He was a colourful character and the residents of Shalom India Housing Society would often remember him for his sense of humour and ready repartee. He was also remembered for almost wrecking Sippora's marriage. But they forgave him when he donated a large sum of money to build a funeral room at the new graveyard of the Jewish community. Even though Raphael had disappeared from their lives, he had a knack of returning to Shalom India Housing Society in other ways. Years later, his photograph appeared in the sports section of various newspapers, as he had been appointed as a choreographer at an international games event. That day, Ezra went from apartment to apartment with the newspaper, telling everybody, 'Look, this is my friend Raphael. You know our Raphael, always dancing and prancing around. Everyone felt he would come to nothing but I always knew he was made for great things. Imagine, if he had stayed on here, he would really have come to nothing. God bless him.'

7

Salome

The Genesis

IT WAS A Wednesday, the first day of Passover. Ezra woke up at 4 a.m. to pray to the sun for Birkat Hachama, when the sun is in the same position that it had been on the day of the Genesis. Saul Ezekiel, the cantor of the synagogue, was to reach the society at 5 a.m.

That morning, Sigaut had already made tea. She was happy that they were living in Shalom India Housing Society, as they could watch the rising sun from their terrace. Ezra had invited the entire Bene Israel community to participate in the prayers and Sigaut had invited them for breakfast in the garden. She had given Salome instructions the night before to make the preparations with Daniyal's help. They had arranged chairs in the garden and bought paper cups for the tea party.

For the prayers, Salome had woken up at 3.30 a.m., had a bath and worn a new sari to greet the sun. It was going to be a long day for her, as Passover was to be celebrated that very evening. She had made preparations the day before with Elisheba, cooking date sheera, which they left in the fridge of the storeroom of the synagogue, along with lettuce and parsley, used as bitter herbs, and Matzo-bread-bhakhris for the Seder table. It had been a long night for both of them and it would be a longer day with the Passover prayers. That night, the cantor had slaughtered a goat according to the law of kosher for the Passover prayers, packed the meat in neat plastic bags and kept it in the fridge. Those who had ordered meat for the week would collect it later in the morning. In the afternoon, Salome and Elisheba would make mutton curry and rice for the Passover table at the synagogue.

Salome enjoyed participating in the Seder at the synagogue with other families. She sighed. Except for a few single women like Ruby and Hadassah, all the houses had families and children. She regretted that she did not have a child. Anyway, she consoled herself, all the children were like her own, especially Sippora's youngest. With a heavy heart, Salome took the elevator to the terrace. It was dark, so Ezra had switched on the light in the anteroom for the Jewish community of the city who trooped in to see the miracle of the sun. Saul Ezekiel was already there with others, their heads covered, facing the skyline, waiting to see the sunrise.

There was silence, as this miracle occurred only once in twenty-eight years. It was believed that on this particular day, the sun would be at the same point in the centre of the horizon as when God created light. It was mentioned in the Jewish Bible, Genesis—I '... And God said, let there be lights in the firmament of the heaven to divide the day from the night... And God made two great lights; the greater light to rule the day, and the lesser light to rule the night:

he made the stars also. And God set them in the firmament of the heaven to give light upon the earth...'

Ezra switched off the terrace light and looked at his wristwatch; it was 5.45 a.m. Saul looked intently at the horizon with a sense of excitement and expectation. He did not want to miss the moment when he could synchronize the time of the sunrise and the prayers. It had to be at the same time. All eyes were glued on the horizon. They could see the silhouettes of other buildings. But as soon as there was a glimmer of brightness on the horizon, a soft, ethereal light enveloped them and they were face-to-face with the sun. Strangely, they felt alone, facing the miracle of creation.

The sun and its golden orb had touched the horizon like the Creator's hand. Saul started reciting a prayer. With every word, the sun rose. The prayer ended in three minutes. The sun was rising from the illusionary line of the horizon, which divided sky and earth. By the time the last line of the prayer was said, the sun was shining in the sky. The moment of magic passed, the sun rose higher, transforming from gold to silver, as the prayer ended with a resounding 'Amen'.

The mystical moment was over. They were engulfed in bright light. Buildings came into focus, street sounds were audible and they heard the call of a golden oriole, which flew over them with a flash of gold, heralding a new beginning.

Salome felt tears sting her eyes. She was going downstairs to make preparations for the tea party when she felt a tiny, warm and sticky hand slide into hers. It was Sippora's son, looking up at her, hiding in the folds of her sari, sucking his thumb. Salome picked him up and kissed him. As the lift door closed, the child snuggled into her arms. She thanked the Lord for small mercies.

8
Ariella

D EAR DANIEL,
 When you receive this letter, you will assume it is a love letter from me. You will be disappointed. I am very angry with you. I did not know you were such a rat. We have been married for twelve years but I have always felt that I did not know you. Take one small example. I spend hours preparing delicious lunches and dinners for you or some unusual recipe for breakfast, but you never appreciate my efforts. You just say, 'It's okay.' And whenever I ask you, 'What would you like to eat today?' your standard reply is, 'Anything.' I have started feeling as if I am just 'anything' in your life. Cleverly, you cover up these shortcomings with a show of affection and gifts, which make me happy and I forget my pain.

 I can never forget that day in September, just before the Jewish New Year, when I was nineteen years old and your family sent a marriage proposal for me while you were in Israel. You had left for Israel when you were maybe fifteen years old. When I saw your date of birth, I realized that you were ten years older than me, but your photograph in your army uniform was impressive. I was hesitant, as I had not seen you in person, but Father said that you belonged to a good family and after your army service you had been employed as a captain in a hotel in Eilat in south Israel.

Your sister Sippora, who lived in Ahmedabad, had seen me in Bombay and felt that we would make a perfect couple. She sent you my photograph, in the same way that I had received yours. A few months later, your father came to meet my parents to apologize that they would have to withdraw the marriage proposal. Your mother wrote to you that I was dark-complexioned, and she wanted a fair-skinned daughter-in-law. Your mother was very proud of the fact that you were fair and looked like a foreigner. Actually, I was relieved, as I did not want to marry someone who had rejected me because of my colour.

I accepted my fate and continued to study the various forms of nail art. I told my parents that I would not see any more suitors from India or Israel.

But a year later, my life was to change. At a bar mitzvah in Bombay, I saw an American staring at me. I assumed he was a Jew, as he was wearing a kippa. I was flattered and started dreaming that we would fall in love and get married. I did not know who he was and did not have the courage to ask anyone to introduce us.

A week later, my mother told me that you were in Bombay for a few days and your father wanted to renew the marriage proposal, as you had seen me at the bar mitzvah. I was confused.

There were so many people there—many young men, some known, others unknown. I could not place you. During a bar mitzvah, the family often invites family and friends from Pen, Panvel, Thane, Alibaug, Ahmedabad, America, Canada and Israel. Maybe you were in the Israeli group, speaking a mixture of Hebrew and Marathi. Anyway, I had torn up your photograph and thrown it away when you had rejected me.

My father convinced my mother after you saw me and liked me. I told my parents, 'I will take a decision after I see him. Now it's my turn. I want to see how fair he is … and if you expect me to go to the beauty parlour, so that I look fair and lovely like the advertisement on television, I will not.'

My parents were worried, as it was not easy to find a husband for me and they had decided that you were the perfect match. When D-Day arrived, I went to my nail-art class and, with a wicked smile, made a scorpion on my thumbnail, hoping that you would see it and reject me. That evening, I did not reach home at the usual time, as I knew that you had been invited at teatime.

All day long Mother tried calling me, but I did not take her calls. I reached home later than usual. I was certain Mother would be upset, as I was dressed in my old jeans and a plain white T-shirt, unlike the last time when I had worn a canary-yellow salwar-kameez with a red dupatta. I did not care because I did not want to marry you.

When Father opened the door, I saw that you were the tall American I had noticed during the bar mitzvah. I was filled with regret. I smiled weakly and went to my room.

There was no time to change as mother was serving tea and samosas. All I did was wash my face, comb my hair and slip on my favourite red heels, just for a touch of colour. In the drawing room, I sat studying you and noticed that you spoke perfect Marathi, like most Bene Israel Jews. Suddenly, I was overcome with anxiety, as I was sure you would reject me a second time.

I liked you. You had nice eyes. You were eating a samosa and watching me. My heart leapt with the hope that eventually we would get married. You seemed to be reading my thoughts because you asked my father if we could go to a nearby café, so that we could get to know each other. The elders agreed.

You were cordial and put me at ease, as I was fidgeting with my hair. Once we had settled down, I felt more confident and asked, 'So, what brings you here? The first time when you received my photograph, you rejected me because of my skin colour.'

'Well, photographs can be deceptive. Last week when I saw you at the synagogue, I was struck by your beauty.'

'I don't believe you.'

'You are very beautiful...'

'But what about my colour...'

'You have a beautiful colour.'

'You are so fair. We would not look good together.'

'It is more important that we like each other.'

'Did you come to see me, consider me, evaluate me, my colour, my looks? You don't have to. Someone like you must have tons of girls falling for you in India and Israel.'

'That is why I am here.'

'What do you mean?'

'Well, a few months back, I was at a friend's home for dinner and his wife asked me what happened about the marriage proposal. I told her the truth. Hearing my reason for refusal, she was very angry and told me that it was unfair to reject a woman without meeting her.'

'So you started feeling guilty and returned to check me out?'

You changed the subject by pointing to the glass counter of pastries and asking, 'Would you like to have a cake?'

'Changing the subject?'

'Not really. I have a sweet tooth.'

'You mean, after all the samosas, you are still hungry?'

'When I arrived at your place with my parents, uncle, nieces, nephews, etc., etc., you were not there, so how would you know how many samosas I had? Actually, I ate because your mother told us you were delayed. And I was sure that you would not turn up. I was nervous and ate all that your mother kept piling on my plate.'

'Ah! That reminds me. I had promised Mother that I would bake a cake. But it just slipped my mind.'

'So I was right. You were trying to avoid me.'

I froze when you asked, 'So you don't like me? You agreed to meet me just to please your parents?'

I looked down at my nails and noticed the scorpion I had painted. I felt a chill pass down my spine. One false move and I could lose you. This was no joke. This was about marriage. I knew many parents from our community were trying to marry their daughters to you. And here I was, behaving like a fool, when you were offering yourself to me on a platter.

So I asked again, 'But what about my colour?'

Desperately, I was trying to hide the fact that I was falling in love with you. With my silly chatter, I was sure I would lose you. I started scraping the scorpion from my nail. That was when I felt you touch my cheek. I looked up, startled, and saw you smiling. I was embarrassed. You misunderstood the startled look and asked, 'Sorry, are you angry...'

I kept silent. I could sense the tension between us. I looked straight into your eyes and said, with a deadpan look, 'I think you would like a brownie!'

'I would... Will you marry me?'

'Yes.'

We left the café, laughing. Our parents were happy on seeing us, as we were holding hands when we entered the house. There was a lot of laughing and kissing. Our families sealed our alliance by feeding sweets to each other and finalizing dates for the engagement and a quick wedding. Everything had to be finalized before your departure. I would follow you once my papers were cleared by the Israeli consulate.

The next day, when we met at the same café, I was dressed in a leaf-green salwar-kameez with a flowing dupatta of the same colour and had worn a subdued shade of lipstick and blue eyeshadow. You held my hand in yours as I asked, 'Do you really like my colour?'

'Yes, I am looking forward to the day we will get married.'

I was pleased, but this doubt stayed with me as long as we were together. It was indicative of our differences, which would come to the fore much later after our wedding and the years we lived together in Israel and India.

Sometimes, jokingly I would ask, 'How come you are so fair?' And you would trace your genealogy to a great-grandfather who had married a Bagdadi Jew, who had been very fair. They had eloped, as in those days there was constant conflict between Bene Israeli Jews and Baghdadi Jews.

To go back to our love story. Once the date for the engagement was finalized, the family waited for your sister Sippora's arrival from Ahmedabad, where she worked as a beautician. I liked her and we bonded easily. When she had seen me for the first time, she had decided that I would make the perfect partner for you. Even after you had rejected me, she had been persistent in trying to get us married.

We had a grand wedding, followed by a glittering reception. Soon after our short honeymoon in Bali, you left for Israel and I followed three months later.

We started life in a small apartment. I learnt Hebrew in an Ulpan. Later, we had two beautiful daughters, Dalia and Orna. We came to India often or our parents came to Israel.

When our daughters were in preschool, I joined a beauty parlour and again learnt nail art from a Chinese beautician in Eilat. I kept myself busy, but sometimes our cold and hot natures clashed.

I noticed that whenever I was frank, you froze and did not speak to me until I apologized and we went back to our peaceful day-to-day existence. It bothered me that every time I said 'sorry' I felt belittled but it pleased you.

But then all love stories have a twist and ours also had one. After ten fairy-tale years, when we had settled down with a few problems here and there, which we sorted out effortlessly, lightning struck our little world.

On our tenth wedding anniversary, we had planned a party at a Kosher Indian restaurant in Tel Aviv. This meant driving from Eilat to Tel Aviv to meet our cousins from both families in time for the party. We often partied at this restaurant, as they had a crooner who mixed Israeli songs with Bollywood numbers. Maybe we would take to the floor as we often did. The interior resembled the film set of a Hindi period movie, with Technicolor curtains, carved arches, tables with lion-paw legs and straight-backed chairs with curved hand rests. And they would keep changing the atmosphere of the restaurant with multi-coloured lights and smoky effects as the music reached a crescendo.

We loved it. Unlike our usual selves, we became overtly romantic whenever we went there and by midnight, when we returned home, we were like a newly-wed couple. But that particular night ended differently.

I remember that evening clearly. I was wearing a royal blue silk sari with a gold border, which I had decided to pair with a heavy pearl bracelet, long dangling earrings and a gold choker—your gift to mark ten years of our married life. While I was fixing the sari-end, you stood in front of the mirror, throwing me appreciative glances and adjusting your turquoise-blue tie over a black shirt. Your cell phone rang. You put it on speaker, as it was a call from India.

It was Sippora. She wished us a happy married life and said she was passing the phone to your parents. Surprised, you asked, 'Are they in Ahmedabad?'

'Yes, they have come to Ahmedabad as Papa is not well.'

'He never told me.'

'It's okay ... nothing to worry about.'

'What happened?'

'He is getting tests done at the hospital ... does not look serious.'

Mamma came on the line, wished us and passed the phone to Papa, who started sobbing, 'I miss you ... my son...'

On the way, always excited about the long drive to Tel Aviv, Dalia and Orna chattered away, but you were silent. Your mood had changed. You felt guilty about leaving your parents in India, although I was sure you were relieved that they were with Sippora. But we had to go through with the party, as we had invited four other couples and their children. That night the party was not as much fun as usual.

When we returned home and went to bed, you said, 'Maybe Papa and Mamma should shift to Ahmedabad permanently. They will not be comfortable in Israel. Remember the last time they were here ... I cannot ask them to emigrate to Israel...'

I kept my silence, as it was one topic which always created tension between us. I leaned over, looked into your eyes, said, 'Happy wedding anniversary,' kissed you, turned on my side and went to sleep. I was afraid something was going to destroy our marriage. I woke up feeling sick.

I had nothing to say in the matter, for your parents often came to stay with us in Israel. During those times, I was overworked with their demands and always on edge as I tried to please them. It was not easy in Israel. Without any help, I had to work, drop and pick up the girls from school, do the shopping, clean the house and do so many other chores, as all Mamma did was dry the washing and find fault with my cooking while Papa sat zapping the channels on television, without understanding a word of Hebrew. In addition, I had to help the girls with their homework. So by the time we went to bed, I was in no condition to talk to you. But you were happy when they were with us.

Sippora often called when I was alone and told me that maybe we would receive phone calls from Papa. We should not worry about these, as he was having memory lapses. He sat on the sofa all day long and had make-believe conversations with you, although Mamma, Sippora, Opher and their children kept reminding him that you were in Israel, not Ahmedabad. Sippora consulted the best doctors in town; Papa did not have a major medical problem. No amount of sedatives helped. He was adamant that he could no longer live without you. Sippora did not want to disturb our family life. She knew that you could take hasty decisions.

Then one day, Papa called you at work, crying and saying that he could not live without you. You came home deeply troubled and left for India that weekend. You returned after a month, looking drawn and confused. That night, you said, 'Maybe it's time we all return to India and live with Papa and Mamma.'

As I left the bedroom to tuck the girls in, I realized you had made a statement, not asked for my opinion. It was not important. When I tried asking about your plans, like job, housing and schooling for our daughters, you snapped back, 'Don't you miss your parents?'

'I do, but now we have a lot at stake here. We do visit India twice a year, or our parents come and stay with us for long periods.'

'Are you trying to say that they outstay their welcome?'

'Not at all. But we do spend more time with them than most people.'

You left the room saying, 'Sippora is there and she will make all arrangements for us ...'

After that, we packed in silence.

Your decision was final.

It was not easy to return to India. We were both earning well, we had fairly decent savings. I knew there would be a problem finding work in India and prepared myself to start from scratch.

I left Israel and bid farewell to friends and relatives. I was heartbroken to have to sell or give away some of my prized possessions. During this period, we were always tense and often fought for no reason at all. Suddenly, we were like strangers.

I was busy, as I had to prepare the girls, who were unhappy leaving their school, friends and activities. And although they spoke fluent English, they were worried about studying in an English-medium school. I only concentrated on them.

We took a flight from Israel to India and went straight to Ahmedabad. Previously we always used to stop over in Mumbai to meet my parents when your parents lived there. But on this trip we did not. I swallowed my hurt.

We arrived at Ahmedabad's Sardar Vallabhbhai Patel International Airport to a warm welcome. The whole family was there to receive us at 2 a.m.

I realized that my days of freedom were over as we all crammed into Sippora's car, hired another taxi and went to her apartment. Most of our bags were stored in A-107 at Shalom India Housing Society. While we were still in Israel, you had met the apartment owner, Juliet, in Ashkelon, given her the year's rent in advance and signed all the necessary papers.

A week later, we settled down in the apartment with your parents. I had the girls admitted to an international school which offered a baccalaureate qualification. We spent a year trying to fit in. And, as I had anticipated, you could not find a job. You spent the day chatting with your father or napping on the sofa in front of the television, with the sports channel always on. You did not help in the house, saying, 'Why do you think we are paying such a fat salary to the cook and the maid?' You were blind to the fact that I did the shopping, chopped vegetables and made chicken curry or fried fish, as the cook only made vegetarian food. Besides this, the girls had to be picked up and dropped, taken to the swimming pool or music classes, where they continued to learn the piano, and also to tuitions to brush up their English. I was so burdened with housework that I did not find time to look for work.

We were growing apart, as we did not spend quality time together. We rarely spoke to each other, except for small household matters or whenever you asked me for a glass of water or cup of tea. I wanted to respond, 'Get it yourself.' But I did not. In the presence of my in-laws, I had to behave like a nice, gentle, well-mannered daughter-in-law.

Our world was shattered. I felt I was your slave.

In a year, I adjusted to my new role. Usually, we went everywhere with Sippora and her family in two cars. But I often faked a headache and stayed home to watch my favourite television serial *Desperate Housewives*, as I was quickly turning into one…

For my own peace, I joined yoga classes and at home, behaved like the deaf-dumb-blind monkeys I had seen at Mahatma Gandhi's ashram during one of our family trips.

One night, things came to a head when we were alone and you held me in your arms. I pushed you away, saying, 'So, when did you start noticing me?'

Embarrassed, you smiled. 'Why? Look, I am the same. I have always been with you.'

'Well, yes, I was your maid all this while. And whenever we were alone in this bedroom, someone or the other always called you at the oddest time. And let me remind you that every single day, even before I had finished all the household chores, you were fast asleep. It was not like back home in Israel when I waited for you, even if you were late, and we spent time together. Here, you don't even notice me...'

You mumbled something like, 'Papa needs me all the time.'

You hugged me and I started crying; you kissed me and I melted in your arms.

The next morning, you were caring and attentive. That evening, you suggested we take a walk and stop at a café. Happily, I agreed. You ordered two cups of cappuccino, samosas and cakes of our choice. That was when you told me that Papa was in bad shape and needed constant medical care. He was in the first stage of Alzheimer's disease. You could not find a decent job, so you had to return to Israel and join your old office. All I could say was, '... and you never told me...'

You said, 'I was not sure about Papa's condition. I came to know about it last week. Yesterday, when he started babbling like a baby, I was sure...'

'It is when you need me that you are attentive, otherwise you are your parents' little boy. So, when are we going back?'

You sipped your coffee, placed the cup back in the saucer and almost blew my mind when you said, 'We are not returning to Israel. I am going back alone. You have to stay with my parents and look after them.' You did not look at me, but kept staring out of the window.

'Great,' I said and pushing away the cup, added, '...but Sippora is here and she is capable of looking after everything. Why should I stay here?'

'Sippora has her own family to look after. As the only son of my parents, it is my duty to look after them.'

'And what about your family...'

At that very moment, Sippora walked in and sat next to me. I thought it was all planned, but she clarified, 'I had gone to meet Papa and wanted to talk to Ariella, when Mamma told me that you were here, so I came to meet you.' When you told Sippora about your decision to return to Israel alone, she retorted angrily, 'It is not necessary for Ariella to stay in India. I am here and we have found a male nurse for Papa.'

But you said, 'I need to return to Israel, earn and support Papa, Mamma and my family. I will come to Ahmedabad twice a year; till then Ariella can be in charge.'

Sippora held my hand. She understood my predicament but was helpless, as once you had made up your mind, it was impossible to talk to you. A week later, you flew to Israel and I went back to my routine.

Before leaving, you gave me a list of instructions, especially about a certain photograph on our bedroom wall. You asked me to remove it. You had taken it when we were in Bali on our honeymoon. You had asked me to wear a bikini when we were on the beach. I was a little shy, but you had insisted that I wear the floral two-piece you had bought in Mumbai before our departure. It was a beautiful photograph and when we settled in Israel, it had pride of place in our bedroom, along with our wedding photo, portraits of Dalia and Orna and one of you floating in the Dead Sea in your swimming trunks, hat on head. These had come with us to Ahmedabad.

When I removed my bikini-clad photograph, I saw that the wall behind it had a discoloured patch. To cover it up, I put the poster of Prophet Elijah, which Juliet had framed and hung on the drawing-room wall. It had always bothered me that since we had moved to Juliet's apartment, the poster had stayed there as part of the decor. We had neither lit a candle for the Prophet, nor organized the ritualistic Eliahu Hannavi prayers, nor held a malida to thank him for our well-being. I moved the poster to my room, prayed to him and asked for help that one day, he would give you enlightenment and we would again live together like a family.

Actually, our bedroom was hardly private. It was a two-bedroom apartment and there was no extra room for us. The room allotted to us was shared with our daughters, who slept on the floor. Now that you had left, I would sleep with our daughters on the same bed.

Before removing it from the frame and putting it away in an old album, I wanted to know why this particular photograph bothered you. After all, it was in our room. To this, you mumbled something about Mamma feeling awkward about it and that the maid often commented on it when she came to clean our room.

On the night of your departure, after dropping you at the airport, I lay awake all night, feeling trapped by your plan of leaving me behind to look after your parents.

In a week, I realized that my workload had tripled and I had much more to do than I had expected. Overnight, I was doing almost everything, as Mamma and Papa sat on the sofa watching television all day. It was then that I worked out a system wherein I could be free for an hour, between cooking, shopping, running the washing machine, drying clothes, picking up and dropping our daughters to school, helping them with homework and taking them for piano classes.

I needed to find relief from the daily grind and joined a beauty parlour. I had befriended the owner, a woman of my age. Around that time, nail art was picking up in Ahmedabad and we included it as part of our parlour services. In a few months, I became known for my designs and young girls started clamouring to get their nails done by me.

Every six months, you returned to Ahmedabad like a good son and responsible father, and you regularly transferred money to our bank account. I kept up pretences in front of your parents, but you knew that I had distanced myself from you. I put an extra mattress on the floor and slept with the girls, making sure to roll up the mattress and put it away before the maid cleaned our room. Although you tried to hold me, embrace me, touch me, I made it clear that I was very angry with you because you had cheated me and I had lost faith in you. This situation continued for more than two years. I was pained that you never discussed the possibility of our return to Israel.

I understood that you managed very well in Israel on your own and had no intention of returning to Ahmedabad. All discussions about our future had stopped. You gave me the impression that you preferred this situation and had decided that we were going to live apart forever. Sippora tried to speak to you but you had stopped confiding in her.

In such a situation, I assumed that you were having an affair in Israel. When I asked Sippora, she said that it was not so. It was just that you were happy with a life without responsibilities. Even when I told you that Papa was stable with medication, Mamma had her own life with her kitty-party friends and Dalia and Orna needed both their parents, my pleas fell on deaf ears.

We lived like this for five years till Dalia and Orna were in their teens. Then I was invited to my niece's wedding in Israel. I informed you that I would be travelling with our daughters and after a long time, we would be together as a family. You said you would receive us when we landed at Ben Gurion Airport. We were happy to see you. You drove us to our old home. But when you opened the door of our apartment, I saw that it was in a total mess. I also noticed that most of your things were not there. You explained that you did not live there anymore. Your office had given you a small apartment in Lod, near your place of work. I was angry and asked why you had not thought it necessary to inform me. You did not answer.

I was disappointed that you did not stay with us. But you came to see us every day. We even went to the wedding together. To all appearances, we were a happy family. That night I told you I would not return to Ahmedabad. You were furious and forced me to return to India. On the flight back, I wanted to cry, but did not. Instead, I decided that I would return and start my own beauty parlour.

Before leaving, I called my Israeli friend Yolam and made arrangements to start the parlour. By the time this letter reaches you, I will be back in Israel, in our apartment, which is also my home, where we first started our life together.

All along, I have always obeyed you.

I even removed my bikini-clad photograph from our room.

I replaced it with the poster of Prophet Elijah.

I prayed to him every day…

He heard my prayers and I am here…

I will start my beauty parlour after having a traditional Thanksgiving malida ceremony for Prophet Elijah with a platter of sweetened poha, dates, apples and bananas, followed by a dinner of chicken biryani and Alphonso mangoes for my friends.

I believe the Prophet has shown me the path to a new beginning. When I had returned to Ahmedabad, every night, before switching off the lights, I would pray to him and miraculously I would see a ray of light from the nightlight fall on his hand as he pointed towards a distant horizon.

Before my departure for Israel, I had taken Dalia and Orna into confidence and lied to Mamma, Papa and Sippora that I was going to Mumbai to meet my parents, as I had not seen them in a long time. Actually, I left for Israel with their help. As a parting gift, my mother gave me a poster of Prophet Elijah. It will have pride of place in my new workplace. One thing is certain; I will not allow you to take decisions for me, nor will I allow you to play with my life. I do not want to be the wife of someone selfish like you. You will receive the divorce papers very soon. But you have the right to meet our daughters. Peace be with you.

Shalom.
Ariella

9

Elisheba

As told to Malkha

DURING PASSOVER, THERE is a favourite chant about the barter of goats, known as Had Gadya, which recounts the story of a goat: 'One little goat ... my father bought for two zuzim. Then came a cat and ate the goat that my father bought for two zuzim. Then came a dog and bit the cat that ate the goat that my father bought for two zuzim. Then came a stick and beat the dog ... my father bought for two zuzim. Then came the fire and burnt the stick that beat the dog that bit the cat that ate the goat that my father bought for two zuzim. Then came the water that doused the fire that burnt the stick that beat the dog that bit the cat that ate the goat that my father bought for two zuzim. Then came the ox and drank the water that doused the fire that burnt the stick that beat the dog that bit the cat that ate the goat that my father bought for two zuzim. Then came the

Shohet and slaughtered the ox that drank the water that doused the fire that burned the stick that beat the dog that bit the cat that ate the goat that my father bought for two zuzim. Then came the angel of death and killed the Shohet that slaughtered the ox that drank the water that doused the fire that burned the stick that beat the dog that bit the cat that ate the goat that my father bought for two zuzim. Then came the Holy One, blessed be; He slew the angel of death that killed the Shohet that slaughtered the ox that drank the water that doused the fire that burned the stick that beat the dog that bit the cat that ate the goat that my father bought for two zuzim.'

But in my story there were two little goats, which my husband Saul had bought for four thousand rupees. All Jewish children like to sing this chant during the Passover Seder. In fact, everybody likes the stanza about the goat that was bought for two zuzim. When it came to this particular chant, the mood changed and the congregation sang with gusto. Like everybody, I also sang it, till I became a character in the episode of the two goats. This episode happened at Reuben's bar mitzvah ceremony when he turned thirteen.

We are only a hundred and forty or fifty Jews in Ahmedabad and such events—bar mitzvahs, circumcisions, malidas and festivals—are few and far between.

That year Reuben celebrated his thirteenth birthday and it was time to include him in the 'minyan' of ten men necessary to hold prayers at the synagogue. Everybody loved Reuben because he had learnt to play the Shofar with Jonathan when he was nine years old. Jonathan, who had been playing the Shofar for the last twenty-four years, had just about mastered it, but Reuben had learnt it quickly. Reuben's parents Nurith and Gideon were proud of their son's proficiency. Sometimes when Jonathan and Reuben played the Shofar one after another, it was hard to believe that the sound was so loud, clear and voluminous.

Reuben is a serious child, good at studies and passionate about cricket, like all Indians. God bless him. His father, Gideon, is a businessman who manufactures machine parts for textile units. He wanted to celebrate Reuben's bar mitzvah in a grand way. The talith or prayer shawl had come from Israel. Reuben's aunt had gifted it to him. She had specially flown in from Israel with her family. Other relatives from Israel, Mumbai and Thane had also come to bless Reuben when he received the prayer shawl.

As the caterer of the community, I had planned the entire menu for the bar mitzvah with Nurith—breakfast, lunch, dinner. I had organized many such events for the Jewish community of Ahmedabad and had often catered for Nurith and Gideon from the time they were married in Mumbai and had their wedding reception in Ahmedabad. Gideon belongs to Ahmedabad and Nurith is one of our many Bombay Brides.

As bar mitzvahs are often held early in the morning, we had planned to serve tea, coffee, biscuits, sandwiches and jalebis, followed by a vegetarian pilaf and ice cream. A break was planned before dinnertime.

And that was the hitch. According to tradition, bar mitzvahs are held on Saturday, the Sabbath; but I had misjudged the problems that could arise when I cooked meat on a Saturday evening. I decided to speak to Nurith about it, but changed my mind. That was my mistake. I should have spoken to her and told her about the difficulties of organizing dinner during the Sabbath, as it is taboo to cook food from Friday evening, when the Sabbath starts, to Saturday night, when it ends. Because of this problem, some families avoid having parties on Saturday night. Instead, they serve a vegetarian meal or organize a festive dinner on Sunday night, which gives enough time to cook meat.

I never told anybody about my anxieties. According to the law, it was not possible for my husband to butcher an animal on Saturday night. It had to be slaughtered on Friday before sunset, then salted and frozen and only cooked on Saturday evening. Till then, it had to stay in the freezer. I was always anxious before I cooked it on Saturday night.

Nothing disastrous had happened so far; there was no need to worry. On that particular day, somehow I was nervous, but started preparations for dinner. During August the weather usually cools down in Ahmedabad, but that year there was a heat wave.

On Friday afternoon, two goats were slaughtered for the Saturday night party. I packed the meat in plastic ziplock bags and froze it in the synagogue refrigerator in the storeroom.

It was not the first time that I was cooking meat on a Saturday night. It was a challenge, as I had to start preparations from Friday night by making the masala. I planned in advance and never failed.

But on Friday morning I had half a mind to call Nurith and tell her that it was advisable to postpone the Saturday dinner to Sunday, so that we could have fresh mutton curry for the party.

I regret that I did not listen to my instinct. Even when my husband slaughtered the animals on Friday according to kosher law, I was distracted and worried. All through Saturday as I organized breakfast and lunch after the bar mitzvah, Reuben strutted around like a rooster in his brand-new prayer shawl. I had checked on the meat in the fridge and wondered why it did not look fresh; it looked pale and dead. I felt there was a stale smell in the room. But I convinced myself that the storeroom always had a musty smell and there was nothing to worry about. It was stacked with old furniture and objects we had received from families when they left for Israel. The fridge was a donation to the synagogue from the Samson family. It was a big double-door frost-free parrot-green fridge, embellished with magnetic stickers. It was already old when it arrived and I had often suggested to the synagogue committee that it be exchanged during the festive season for a new one. But Simon had checked it and given his verdict that it worked very well. Since then, we used it to freeze chicken, mutton or vegetables. So far it had never let us down. It was also not for the first time that we had frozen meat for almost two days. I closed the fridge, went downstairs to the kitchen and busied myself in preparing the mutton curry. I browned the finely chopped onions as my daily help washed the meat and then I sautéed it in the red masala till it had a nice red colour.

An hour later, I forked the meat to see if it was cooked, then added a large quantity of coconut milk, simmered it for fifteen minutes more and garnished it with finely chopped coriander leaves. But somewhere in the back of my mind, I was wondering why it did not exude the aromatic fragrances it normally did. To distract myself, I made a cauldron of rice and tossed a salad of cubed cucumber, tomatoes and onions with lemon juice.

My fears proved true when the food was served. There was chaos in the synagogue pavilion. Lebana was the first to fill her plate. She had a morsel, made a face and whispered to her sister that the meat was stale. Like lightning, the message passed from one to the other and reached Nurith and Gideon. They noticed that nobody was eating. Then Nurith filled her plate to reassure the guests that all was well and ate a spoonful. Her face contorted with disgust as she called out to me, 'Elisheba, the meat is stale…' I froze. The otherwise mild-mannered Nurith was telling me that I had ruined her son's bar mitzvah dinner.

I stood with bent shoulders as the truth sunk in. Not one to panic, I called out to my eldest son and asked him to buy paneer masala and dal fry, available at the corner restaurant near the synagogue. I made sure that he raced on his motorbike. At that moment, I saw Nurith making preparations to leave the venue but begged her to stay, telling her that I had made other arrangements. I stood in the doorway and announced that I would not allow anybody to leave the synagogue on an empty stomach. In the meantime, I opened packets of potato chips and served cold drinks.

Meanwhile, my husband went to the storeroom to check the fridge. His heart sank when he saw that it was not working. Shamefacedly, he came down, stood beside me and whispered, 'It is nobody's fault. The fridge is not working.'

Making sure that I was heard, I said, 'When we prepared the meat on Friday evening, the fridge was working. Then, because it was the Sabbath, I did not go into the storeroom. This evening when I took out the meat from the fridge to cook it, I did not notice that the fridge was not working. I apologize. It is my fault.'

The congregation sat still as I carried the vessels back into the kitchen. My son arrived with packets of food and I laid it on the table. By then, Nurith had calmed down and offered to pay for the food. I refused.

Our home is next to the synagogue, so I rushed home and packed a gift for Reuben. After everybody had eaten well, I called Reuben and gave him the gift for his bar mitzvah.

The next day, when Nurith and Gideon opened the gifts, I am sure they must have been thunderstruck. I had given Reuben two silver coins, my life's savings.

Soon, the matter of the stale meat was forgotten, but the memory of the silver coins would remain with me forever. I had given the coins to Reuben as I did not want to tarnish my reputation.

This is how Reuben received two silver coins on his bar mitzvah, because, after all, it was just a matter of two zuzim.

10

Malkha

As told to Elisheba

T RY AS I might, I cannot eat fish. Imagine a woman from Alibaug, who comes from the land of the fish-eating Bene Israel Jewish community, getting put off by the mere smell of fish. I call it 'smell', although it is the best fragrance on earth. However, as a child, I enjoyed going to the Alibaug fish market with Mother, where fish was brought fresh from the sea, and identifying the different types. Pomfret is as dear to a Jewish woman's heart as Bombil or Bombay Duck, which I liked, because when it arrived from the sea, it had a rose-pink colour with a touch of white and looked like a flower. It is delicious when rubbed with rice flour and deep fried till golden-brown, but now I cannot bear to look at it. I wonder why?

From a very young age, I was taught that we were only allowed to eat fish with scales yet, at the fish market, I was often attracted to shrimps, prawns, lobsters and crabs, with their soft flesh encased in hard armour. I would have a great desire to open the shells and feel the sweetness inside, which my friends and neighbours had told me about. But I never ate fish without scales, because it was taboo in our religion.

All was well, as long as I was unmarried. A month after my wedding to Samson, I was alone one afternoon and marinating fish in salt and lemon juice, when I suddenly felt nauseated. I cooked it anyway and quickly made some spinach for myself, which I had bought for the evening dinner. When Samson saw me eating spinach and not touching the fish, he asked me why. I avoided telling him the truth. I told him that I sometimes preferred leafy vegetables to chicken, meat and fish. He gave me a quizzical look, but did not say anything.

After Samson's demise, I moved to Ahmedabad to live with my son Ezel, daughter-in-law Tamar and their children Amy and Benny in his apartment A-109 at Shalom India Housing Society. But when Ezel and Tamar decided to emigrate to Israel, I returned to my house in Alibaug. When Tamar separated from Ezel, I helped my son, looking after the house and children. But when she returned to India, I went back to Alibaug. I will always value the memory of having spent time with Ezel, Benny and Amy. Maybe I have got used to living without Ezel, but not Amy. I miss her sweet chatter, as she liked to snuggle into the folds of my sari and tell me about her school friends and any children's story she had read at the school library.

Once Tamar returned to Ezel's life, he did not discuss their plan of leaving for Israel, but I heard him telling his friends that he had booked four air tickets. Rather hurt, I asked him to book my train ticket to Alibaug. I was sad, but happy that Ezel and Tamar were together again. I returned to Alibaug with a heavy heart.

When I reached, I opened the front-door lock of my home, dreading the endless lonely hours I would have to spend there. I had informed my old caretaker Sonbai about my arrival, and she was waiting for me at the door. I opened the windows, aired the house, dusted and cleaned it, washed the kitchen shelves, ordered a fresh stock of groceries from the shop down the road, washed the vessels, wiped them clean, polished the brass vessels, asked Sonbai to clean the floor, beat the dust out of the mattresses, changed the bed sheets, called the dhobi and gave him a huge mound of washing, rearranged the furniture, carried my favourite deck-chair to the veranda and made a cup of hot tea for myself. My heart warmed when the mongrel Brownie, whom I had brought up when he was a pup, returned, wagging his tail. Sitting there, I watched the coconut trees in the front yard and made notes of the things I had to do, such as ask a farmer to look after the trees and help with the marketing of the coconut harvest, subscribe to a newspaper and ask the local veterinary doctor to give shots to Brownie. As he licked my feet, I felt I had returned home. It was then that my aversion towards fish reemerged and I did not know how to handle it. So I tried to jog my memory and remember my family history, which I had heard from my mother, aunts, ageing cousins and grandmother. I could not put my finger on the root of the matter. I vaguely remembered that this feeling went way beyond the stories of a grand-aunt and my great-grandmother. I was sure something had happened to one of the women before them. I wondered why it was so deeply ingrained in my memory for as far as I could remember, it had not bothered any of the other women in my family, but had disrupted my world.

Living alone, I had a lot of time on my hands, so I tried to grow vegetables in my backyard, and made sure that the coconut and areca-nut trees were looked after. I also checked on the harvest and began maintaining an account book of returns. In the afternoon, I met old friends and took an hour-long nap. Twice a week, I worked as a volunteer in the local library and brought back novels, which I read before falling asleep at night.

In contrast, my Friday evenings were spent in a state of agitation after I attended the Sabbath prayers at the synagogue in Israel Lane. I returned home soon after, ate a hasty meal of leftovers from lunch and sat next to the telephone, abstractedly watching the news in Marathi. At around 10 p.m. my eyes would wander to the old grandfather clock on the wall, above my wedding photograph, as around that time Ezel would call me. Our conversations were always short, followed by the excited shouts of Amy and Benny. Then Ezel would return to the phone and end the conversation with his statement that it was the children's bedtime. Once I heard the click of the phone being put back on the holder, I would return to my bedroom with a heavy heart, feeling an oppressive loneliness. I fretted about the fact that my daughter-in-law Tamar never spoke to me. So I spent an uneasy night on Fridays. Yet I did not want to tell Ezel that it was hard to live alone, without any direct family in Alibaug.

As if that was not enough, I became obsessed with fish of all kinds and colours. These often turned into nightmares—when tiny fish with shiny scales transformed into enormous whales and almost swallowed me up, like the Biblical tale of Jonah and the whale. That was when I would invariably wake up at around 2.30 a.m. in a sweat. I tried to fall asleep again, but could not, so I counted whales, in the way that one counts sheep and falls asleep. At 7 a.m. I would wake up with a start, when the milkman called out to me, make my morning tea and sit on the veranda and read *The Raigadh Times*, before starting my day.

One such year, there were heavy rains in Alibaug and I had to stay home, however much I disliked it. That morning, I made a simple lunch of dal and rice, ate it while watching my favourite Marathi serial, rested and then pulled out the old bags and tin trunks stacked in various places of the house, having decided to clear up unnecessary baggage. Just then I heard someone rattle the main gate of the house. I opened a window and saw the fishmonger Durga, who went from house to house selling fish, which she carried in a huge basket on her head. It was covered with an enormous plastic sheet, which enveloped her entire body. Seeing her standing there, I had a strong desire to have fried fish for dinner. I knew Durga well and asked her to come to the veranda. She squatted on the floor and uncovered the fish. I saw that she had a good catch of pomfret. But as soon as she held one up to show how fresh it was, I again felt a deep aversion for my favourite fish and wanted to throw up. Much to Durga's shock, I refused to buy it and closed the door. Not that I wanted to be rude, but I was afraid I would vomit right there on the basket of fish. From behind the door, as Durga covered her basket with the plastic sheet, I heard her murmur, 'Strange woman, never know when she wants fish and when she doesn't...'

Feeling sick, I lay down for an hour. Later, when I was better, I pulled out an old tin trunk from under my bed and tried to open the rusted lock. Unsuccessful, I asked Sonbai, who had just walked in, to help me. She oiled it, turning its bolts with its enormous key. As she turned the key in the other direction, the lock opened with a loud click.

I spent the entire week discarding old, mouldy papers from the trunk. That is when I came across an old hand-stitched diary, which was torn and discoloured with time. Some pages were stuck to each other and I was afraid they would tear. The writings were in old Marathi and although it was damaged, some of it was readable.

That evening, I put on my spectacles, sat at the dining table and started reading while listening to the rain pounding on the roof. As it often happened in Alibaug, the electricity kept fluctuating, so I lit a hurricane lantern, which I kept on a table near my chair, and got totally absorbed in the interesting details of my family history.

At first I thought it was just an account of daily life and expenses, written in a clean floral hand by my great-great-great grandmother with the unusual name of Delilah. I wondered what she had looked like. Luckily I found a photograph of those years in another trunk, where I had stored ancient, faded sepia-tinted family photographs.

Studying the photographs, I was fascinated by one particular face. I do not know if I was right, but I was convinced that it was Delilah. In comparison to the other women, she was thin and tiny with a long vixen-like face. She was dressed in a nine-yard Maharashtrian sari, and wore a nose ring much larger than the lower part of her face, heavy silver anklets with a serpentine design, a broad armlet with silver bells, innumerable glass bangles and a waistband, which showed off her tiny waist to advantage.

I sighed and wished that I was half as beautiful as Delilah. I looked at myself in the mirror and the face looking back at me was plain and ordinary.

Like Jonah, it took me three days and three nights to read the old Marathi script, as it took longer to understand some of the words. It was during this time that I came across a part which clarified my issues. It was late in the night, so I put a bookmark on that page, placed the diary next to my pillow and slept.

The next morning, Sonbai cooked a simple meal for me and I sat all day at the dining table, reading the diary. The rains were receding and I could hear the soft roar of the sea. Delilah had written,

… that month, it had rained continuously and we could not go out to buy fish—we would cook fish every day, either for lunch or dinner. So we had to survive on dal, rice, yoghurt, potatoes or any vegetable we could buy at a high price from the farmers living around our house. Besides that, we always had wheatflour, rice flour, chick-pea flour, rice and pickles. We also made a chutney of onions, garlic, sesame seeds, dry red chillies and salt, which we ate as an accompaniment to most foods. From the storeroom of the house, we tried to make a variety of

interesting dishes. We had a good stock of dried Bombay Duck, but one morning, we woke up to the stench of rotting fish, as it had spoilt because of the humidity. We had to throw away our precious bags of Bombay Duck in the manure pits of our fields. That afternoon, when the rains receded, I took my bamboo umbrella and went to the fish market with my elder son, hoping to find a small quantity of fish, for which I was prepared to pay a high price. There was knee-deep slush around the fish market, so I hitched up my sari to reach there. When I reached, I saw a scene I can never forget. The fishermen and their families stood in small groups, wailing, crying and beating their chests, as though they were at a funeral. Gradually, I understood that when the rains receded, the fishermen had gone fishing but had returned with dead fish. From a distance, I saw that the entire surface of the sea was covered with dead fish, the stench of which hung over Alibaug like a dark cloud. That month, we had to go without fish.

I was impressed by Delilah's graphic narration. I was so obsessed with the diary that I rushed through the morning chores, made a simple lunch with Sonbai, had a bath, ate, took a nap, wiped my spectacles and read on,

... Bene Israeli Jews crave fish. Whatever else we may have for lunch or dinner, we always have the desire for even an inch of fried fish or a slice of pomfret in rich red curry served with a mound of rice on our thalis. So the absence of fish caused a vacuum in our lives. But at the end of that month, one night, we woke up with a start. There were shouts and cries coming from the direction of the sea. Although, it was still raining, the men took their umbrellas and ran towards it. We sat huddled on the veranda, until a neighbour returned and informed us that a

huge whale had been washed up on the beach. The British officer stationed there said that it was a white whale. We were curious to see it, so when the men returned, we made a hasty meal and went to the seashore to see the huge fish, which was still alive and breathing. She looked like a white mountain, obstructing our view of the sea. At first we were afraid to go closer, as we were sure she would swallow us. She lay there for ten days and every day, we went to look at her. Slowly, we inched closer to her. There were always big crowds around her, but we went nearer so that we could have a good view of this enormous creature which had erupted from the sea, elusive, yet attractive. We wanted to touch her. As for me, I was fascinated by her round head, large eyes and lips, which opened and closed as she sucked in air, making her look like a baby.

Maybe at that moment I sinned, as I started salivating and wondering why the Lord had sent such a big fish into our lives, when we were only craving for a small piece to satiate us. At that moment, I forgot all our dietary laws instilled in me as a child by my mother and later my mother-in-law. All I wanted to do was go close to this enormous mass of fish-flesh, claw it, take a huge chunk and rush home. I would cook it, serve it to the family and eat a piece. For me, it was like nectar that had been sent to us, maybe by the Lord.

I stopped reading, as it was getting dark. I was hungry and my eyes were paining with the strain. I was about to close the diary, when I saw that some pages were torn and there were marks on the pages, which appeared to be tear stains. So I washed my eyes, sat down, wore my spectacles and continued reading, when my eyes froze on one word on a torn page, '...*sinned*...'

I could not figure out if Delilah had gone to the beach alone when nobody was around, approached the fish with a sharp cleaver, hacked a piece of its tail, taken it home, cooked it, fed the family and eaten it herself. Or did she have it all alone in a corner of a field, where she cooked it on a wood fire? This, I assumed, was the meaning of the single word '...*sinned*...'

The next day, I again hurried through my chores and sat down to read Delilah's diary. I was confused, as there were disconnected lines on torn pages:

'... *this fish on the seashore, which looks as big as a house, had died. It was buried on the beach ... a few months later ... it erupted like a volcano ... there was a lot of destruction ... some fishermen's huts were destroyed... I was distressed and held myself responsible for its death ... since then I cannot eat fish...*'

I now started understanding my inability to eat fish. I closed the diary, went to bed early and woke up when the milkman called out to me. Then I went back to bed and woke up much later, when Sonbai rang the doorbell.

After reading Delilah's diary, I became a vegetarian. Two years later, a similar white whale was washed ashore on the Alibaug beach on a rainy night and I was dragged back into the diary, her agony and torture. So many years later, I was living through her pain.

I spent all my time in the library, reading about whales in old *National Geographic* volumes, stacked in a corner, which I dusted and arranged according to their dates. A young reader saw my interest in whales and advised me to install cable television, on which I could see films on whales and wildlife. So I found a cable operator, who installed more than ninety channels on my television set. This made my life more interesting, as when I was not reading about whales and marine life, I was watching films about wildlife. In the process, I gathered an enormous amount of information, which I noted in my diary, sitting in my favourite chair on the veranda.

During this period, I read in the newspapers that the forest department officials were trying to save the whale. The report said that it was a young whale, about two years old, and they were making great efforts to release her back into the sea. But she was badly injured, maybe by a whale-hunting trawler, and was dying, as she was stuck in a ditch. After she had breathed her last, she was buried in a distant corner of the seashore. This created another problem, as with time, there was an unbearable stench. To solve this problem, a kind doctor living in the vicinity unearthed her carcass with the help of the forest rangers and invited experts from Mumbai to clean and treat her bones, which were reconstructed and displayed in a shed near his house. I befriended the doctor and his family and participated in the entire process. Interestingly, this became a major attraction for the locals and weekend tourists who came to Alibaug.

Two years later, another adult whale was washed ashore on Alibaug beach and I was agonized. But by then, I was better prepared as I had read everything about whales and what happened to them if they were stranded on a seashore. During my research, I had found the clue to Delilah's whale. From the details I had gathered from her story, I came to the conclusion that when Delilah's whale had died and was buried on the seashore, as often happens with the corpses of whales, it emitted innumerable toxic gases, which burst out of the ground like a volcanic eruption. I assumed that something like this must have happened, causing death and destruction in the village of the fisherfolk who lived there. I was sure this had given Delilah mixed feelings of guilt, sorrow and sin, as she held herself responsible for the whale's death and the ensuing death of some fishermen she had known.

Delilah's secret sorrow had floated towards me through the ages, like a supernatural being, along with the spirit of the whale whose flesh she had carved. Maybe she had slashed the whale's tail, fin or tongue, the only edible parts, which would look similar to the fish they regularly ate. This distant event had entered into me, creating a love-hate relationship with all kinds of fish.

I understood Delilah better through her diary, which had also led to my new-found knowledge of whales. Once I understood her and all that she had gone through, I readied myself to face the present situation. So, every morning, I woke up feeling content, not alone and troubled. I realized that this particular whale had given a new meaning to my life. I felt a great love for the sea and all those big and small creatures that lived in its underbelly.

I realized that I had also stopped waiting for Ezel's Friday night phone calls. In fact, whenever he called, I told him and the children stories about whales and their family life. They were amused by my obsession with sea life, but something told me not to mention Delilah and how it had all started. Somewhere, I was still hurt about how Tamar had reacted when I was in Alibaug and had cut down a coconut tree and found its heart, which was locally known as 'Oti Chi Poti'—a sign of good luck, the size of my ring finger, as sweet as the core of a half-opened coconut. I had packed it in muslin and taken it all the way from Alibaug to Ahmedabad as a gift for Ezel, Tamar, Amy and Benny. But Tamar had been suspicious about the 'Oti Chi Poti' and my intentions when I gave a small piece to Amy to taste. She had accused me of trying to poison the child, grabbed it from my hand and thrown it into the dustbin. And Ezel, who had grown up eating it, had remained silent, seemingly siding with his wife. Since then, I had chosen not to tell Ezel anything related to village life. In fact, whenever Ezel spoke to me, I was always afraid that he kept his cellphone on speaker so that Tamar could hear my conversation with them.

A few years later, again during a heavy monsoon, another whale appeared on the beach. She was stuck in a ditch but she appeared to be in good health. Even as the fisher folk living along the shore informed me about her arrival, the chief conservator of forests of

Raigadh district called me and told me about the whale. By now almost everybody knew about my interest in whales. He invited me to join his staff in rescuing the whale and returning it to the sea. I decided to be at the forefront of the activity. I even bought myself a pair of jeans and wore Ezel's old kurta.

I felt self-conscious in my new attire, but the whale was more important than appearances and I did not want to go wading through the water in a cumbersome sari.

The first two days, a lot of people took 'selfies' on their cellphones and children even climbed upon the whale. 'Operation Save the Whale' took place when there was a high tide, supposed to be the perfect time to release a stranded whale into the sea. I named her Delilah. She was lifted carefully with an earth-mover and released back into the sea. I had tears in my eyes as I stood on top of a forest department truck and saw her slowly slide into the water, take a deep breath, release a spurt of water and with a slow lyrical movement like a dancer, float towards the high seas, cut through the waves and disappear into the golden horizon of the evening sky.

The forest department jeep dropped me home. I opened the lock of the front door, exhausted, drank a glass of cold water, changed into my nightgown, lay down and slept peacefully for the first time in years.

11

Golda

It was my first encounter with a matchmaker. We Indian Jews need them, as in our small community, it is difficult to find the right match. Lately, many young people are getting married outside the community, so now we have quite a few matchmakers, as parents want their children to marry Jews. Actually, I liked this man who fixed marriages on earth, not in heaven, so I named him Matchmaker Uncle.

We live in Alibaug, across the sea from Mumbai, so my parents had asked a matchmaker from Mumbai to find me a suitor. I was against it. So far the young men who had come to 'see' me had rejected me. I had come to terms with it and was happy working as a music teacher in an English-medium school in Alibaug. I was highly regarded there because I was a trained vocalist in the Hindustani classical style. But I had to go through the torturous process of my candidature as a would-be-bride. What I had accomplished was impressive, and moreover, I was named after Golda Meir, the first woman prime minister of Israel. My photograph, taken at the local studio, did not reveal my flaws. Yet, it always happened that as soon as a would-be-groom came face-to-face with me, he would immediately refuse to even consider me. The reason was that I was born with fine down on my face and all over my body. Mother tried rubbing my skin with a rough towel, but it did not help; it only gave me a rash. Later, as a teenager, she sent me to a beauty parlour, but again I came back with a severe allergy, which lasted six months. The doctor warned my parents that doing any kind of beauty treatment would give me a lifelong skin problem. While every other girl looked beautiful after a visit to the beauty parlour, I was doomed to look ugly. So, I was surprised that the matchmaker had found a suitor for me despite having been told all about my problem. I was sure that even after all his efforts, one look at me and the suitor would refuse.

As always, I was depressed on the day the suitor was to arrive. My father had told me that he was Moses from Ahmedabad. He had already been convinced by Matchmaker Uncle that I would make a perfect wife for him. He had also been told that I was not beautiful in the conventional sense, but was a good, homely girl with a small problem, which he could see for himself. This clause relieved me, as both of us could escape from the impending marriage. Till then I had not been told that the suitor also had a flaw.

Moses was a booking clerk at the computerized section of the Ahmedabad railway station, a simple man looking for a homely wife. He had no other demands. I was told that he had been brought up by his paternal aunt who had recently died. He wanted to get married; all he needed was a companion. He had lost his mother when he was fifteen and his father at twenty. So his father's unmarried sister, who had been living with them, took care of him. Moses had a degree in computer science, so when his aunt retired as a railway booking clerk, he got her job. She also tried to get him married but for some reason or the other, she was not successful.

Some girls found him too simple and he rejected many for being too fashionable. And, knowing his preferences, Matchmaker Uncle had convinced him that I would be the perfect choice for him. He had also told my parents that Moses did not mind if his future wife continued working as a schoolteacher. He had assumed that I taught English at a primary school in Alibaug and did not ask for details.

Everything appeared to be perfect, but I had my reservations. I knew that one look at the fine growth on my upper lip and I would not be acceptable to Moses. Maybe he would leave immediately for Ahmedabad.

Matchmaker Uncle had informed my parents that Moses lived in a rented apartment in Shalom India Housing Society, A-106. The owners, an elderly couple, were in Israel, where they had a flat, so they often commuted between the two countries. Moses had set up a temporary home there, as he had had to vacate his apartment in the government housing society, which had been allotted to his aunt years ago. They had levelled out the old society and were building a high-rise. When it was ready, we would move to an apartment there. So, if we got married, we would live in the apartment at Shalom India Housing Society.

I had gone through so many rejections that my mother did not force me to dress up or wear make-up. My parents allowed me to wear whatever I wanted to. On that particular day, I chose a dark-blue salwar-kameez with a purple paisley design, a printed dupatta, a wristwatch and silver earrings, which, incidentally, my elder sister had bought from Ahmedabad, when she was there for a wedding. I liked them. And, of course, much against my mother's suggestion to leave my hair open, as it suited my face, I annoyed her by oiling and braiding it, because I was sure I was going to be rejected. Mother kept her silence. I knew she thanked the Lord that it had been easier to get my elder sister married to a Mumbai businessman. My sister had a flawless complexion and no problems.

Matchmaker Uncle had given us Moses's passport-size photograph, saying that he was around thirty years old. I saw he had a long face, small eyes, a receding chin and thinning hair. While I was fairly good-looking with aquiline features, a good singer and a fun-loving person, Moses looked serious.

When Moses arrived to 'see' me with Matchmaker Uncle, I scrutinized my groom-to-be while Mother bustled around serving tea and biscuits. He was not tall; maybe we were of the same height. He was wearing a full-sleeved white shirt over gray trousers. When he entered, he shook hands with me and looked at me. After that, he never looked in my direction and I felt strangely relieved that he had already rejected me. As he sat on the sofa, drinking tea and talking to my parents, I assumed that maybe he had good eyesight and in one look he had noticed everything about me.

Eventually, Moses and Matchmaker Uncle left to catch the last boat to Mumbai. According to tradition, these decisions took long. I hoped we would receive a refusal. But the next evening Matchmaker Uncle called my father to say that Moses had approved of me and would like to get married as soon as possible. When my father announced, 'Moses has agreed to marry Golda,' I was shocked, as I had had no say in the matter.

I told my parents, 'At least ask me if I want to get married to Moses!'

My mother brusquely told me, 'I am not asking you anymore. At last a young man wants to marry you and you will… Look, once we are gone, do you want to live like an ageing spinster in your sister's house all alone…?'

So, with a sinking heart, like a goat being led to the slaughterhouse, I accepted their verdict. My father ordered boxes of pedas to be distributed amongst relatives, neighbours, friends and the Jewish community of Alibaug. My parents felt a sense of victory that at last they had found a groom for me.

While the festivities were going on, I asked my mother to meet me alone in my room. I locked the door and, pointing to the down on my upper lip, asked her angrily, 'Before you go ahead with the announcement, please make sure that Moses has agreed to marry me. Because he never looked at me properly, as I was sitting near the curtain and he did not notice … my … my problem…' I looked at her with tear-filled eyes. Mother was moved and immediately called Father. They retreated to their bedroom and called Matchmaker Uncle, who confirmed that Moses had accepted me with all my flaws. When Mother repeated his words to me, I was hurt. I felt I was being pushed into an unknown area, maybe a blind alley…

So far, my life in Alibaug had been predictable and familiar with the sea around me, fishing boats with colourful sails, the changing shades of the sky, fresh chiki simmering in cauldrons of jaggery, tall coconut trees, lush green rice fields, a bustling market, umpteen varieties of fish, the graves of our ancestors, the Magen Aboth Synagogue—where we prayed like one big family—and the Rock of Prophet Elijah or Eliahu-Hannabi-cha-Tapa in Sagav village. For a second, I prayed to the Prophet to whisk me away in his chariot, so that I could disappear and not have to marry Moses. But nothing like that happened.

Before Moses arrived, life in Alibaug meant laughter and sharing food with friends and neighbours. Yes, I was not like the heroine who advertised a fairness cream on television, but I was popular in my school because I was a trained vocalist in the Hindustani classical style, had a good voice and entertained family and friends with ghazals, old and new Hindi film songs or Konkani folk songs. And, at Jewish gatherings, I was often invited to sing kirtans in Marathi based on Biblical themes, as I had inherited my grandmother's book of kirtans, which was based on narratives of the Patriarch Moses receiving the Ten Commandments and the ascent of Prophet Elijah to heaven. These were some of my happy moments, when my audience applauded and often gave me a standing ovation. During such moments, I was not weighed down by my spinster status. Through the years, I had come to terms with my fate. Then Moses arrived and my life changed forever. For reasons I never understood, Matchmaker Uncle, who knew about my singing talents, had advised my parents to hide this fact from Moses. So, when Moses sent his approval, my parents explained to me that he might disapprove of a girl known for her talents. I would have to give up singing for a while…

At that very moment, I was humming a tune under my breath. I stopped singing and felt suffocated. It was as if someone had taken the life out of me. I was also annoyed with my parents, for in their enthusiasm to get me married, they did not consider my feelings. They were happy to have found a suitor for me.

Singing was my only passion and as they gave me instructions, I gasped, crumpled into the sofa-chair, raised my voice and told them that I would not stop singing. My parents were worried that I would refuse the marriage proposal and lose my last chance of being wedded. They were also worried that I would fall in love with a non-Jew and have a runaway marriage. I felt trapped and reluctantly accepted the proposal.

I again prayed to Prophet Elijah, asking him to help me escape from this situation. It was then that I saw my harmonium, which had pride of place in the drawing room. So, much to my parents' displeasure, I said rather sarcastically that I would marry him only if I could take my harmonium with me.

Matchmaker Uncle asked Moses and surprisingly he agreed, but on the condition that I would not practise singing at home. But I could if and when I worked as a schoolteacher in Ahmedabad. So in a subtle way Moses was informed that I was a music teacher.

With these agreements, I was married to Moses at the Magen Aboth Synagogue in Alibaug. As Moses did not have family in

India, he came with Ezra, the president of Shalom India Housing Society, where he lived. I was married in the presence of the small Jewish community of Alibaug. This was followed by an ice-cream party in the courtyard of the synagogue. The next day we were to leave for Ahmedabad.

To make the wedding memorable, my mother and her friends decorated my bedroom with flowers. She also joined the two divan beds in my room and covered them with a floral rose-pink bedsheet.

That night, there was a teary farewell in our drawing room. Naturally, I also cried. I dreaded entering my bedroom. I need not have worried, as Moses, wrapped in a shawl, was sleeping on the farthest corner of the bed.

The next day, after breakfast, we left for Ahmedabad in a station-wagon taxi, booked by Matchmaker Uncle, who had decided to take the expressway to Ahmedabad, as it would be more convenient with my bags. If we had left by catamaran from Alibaug to Mumbai, I would have had to leave behind some of my belongings. As it was a big car, Matchmaker Uncle and Ezra made themselves comfortable in the seats behind the driver, while I sat with Moses in the backseat. Throughout the journey, the men chatted as though I did not exist, so I watched the changing landscape. I was pleased that I had had my way and my harmonium was packed in a box right behind me in the taxi.

When we reached Shalom India Housing Society late that night, we were given a warm welcome by some families who were waiting for us. I was tired but politely shook hands with everybody. Daniyal, the caretaker of the society, and others helped Moses carry the bags to the elevator, and Daniyal's wife, Salome, accompanied me to Moses's apartment, my new home. Ezra's wife Sigaut sent us vegetarian biryani and told me that they would be there for the wedding reception Moses had organized on the lawns of Shalom India Housing Society. I assumed that Moses had forgotten to tell me about it, so I smiled and entered the apartment without ceremony. I needed a shower and change of clothes. As soon as my bags came up, I took my nightclothes and was happy to disappear into the bathroom. But before that I carried my harmonium to what looked like an unused bedroom, next to Moses's master bedroom, and pushed it under the divan bed, covering it with a dupatta I had pulled out from my bag. I then took out a lace-trimmed nightdress, which my mother had insisted I wear on my first night with Moses.

Later, when Moses came in, he gave me an extra bunch of keys to the flat and explained some basics about the kitchen, the cooking gas, the geyser in the bathroom. He told me to keep the balcony doors closed, as langoors often raided the flat. I told him I would manage. Then he went into the bedroom, showered, changed into his pyjamas and came straight to the dining table as if it was the most natural thing on earth. I had laid the table with two plates, spoons and the biryani. He ate hurriedly and went back into the bedroom, where he switched off the lights.

I collected the dishes, put them in the kitchen sink and kept the leftovers in the fridge, as I did not see any other food in the house. I then filled a bottle of water for myself and stood at the bedroom door watching Moses. He had switched on the ceiling fan and was sleeping in the same way he had slept on my bed in Alibaug. He had left place for me to sleep next to him. The bed looked as though it was divided in two. There was a pillow and a shawl for me…

I stood at the door, feeling like an intruder. The apartment was a mess. I was troubled that Moses had not made any effort to make me feel welcome in our new home. I consoled myself that maybe he had been in a hurry to reach Alibaug for the wedding and had not had the time to make the flat liveable. Maybe he was exhausted.

I blessed Sigaut for the food she had sent. Anticipating this situation, my mother had also packed boxes of dry snacks, aloo parathas and sweets, otherwise we would have slept on an empty stomach. I froze the parathas in the fridge, in case we would need them for the next day's lunch. I did not know what to expect of Moses. I peeped into the bedroom, saw that he was fast asleep and decided not to enter. I switched off the lights and made myself comfortable in the smaller bedroom. I lay down on the narrow divan bed and slept, feeling comforted by the harmonium next to me.

Next morning, I woke up to the insistent ringing of the doorbell. I sensed that Moses was not in the apartment, so I rushed to open the door. A boy in his late teens was standing there. He said that he cleaned Moses Saab's flat every morning. He was Franco Fernandez's full-time help, but also worked as a part-time cleaner for others. He offered me a rose, saying, 'Shaadi mubarak, Madam,' congratulating me on my wedding. Touched by his gesture, I thanked him, placed the flower in a glass of water and busied myself in the kitchen. I looked in the fridge and saw that there was no milk, but by then Moses was back as his help greeted him with 'Shaadi mubarak' as well. Moses left two packets of milk, a loaf of bread and butter on the counter and sat at the dining table reading the newspaper, waiting for tea. Then he dressed and, before leaving for work, stopped at the door saying, 'I have organized a wedding reception downstairs at 7. I have invited everybody from our community and some friends from my office. The caterers and decorators will look after everything. I will be back by 4 in the afternoon.'

When the doorbell rang again, it was Salome. She offered to help me organize the apartment, as she knew where Moses kept the linen. Together, we changed the bedsheets and curtains, so that the house looked presentable. While I was cleaning the fridge, she showed me a cupboard where Moses kept basic provisions. He hardly ever cooked, eating at his office canteen or ordering food from a tiffin service in Block B. She offered to send me lunch but I told her there was enough food in the fridge. By the time she left

I had understood the geography of the apartment. I saw that there were only two photo frames on the walls, one of Moses's late aunt and the other of the Prophet Elijah in his chariot.

Then I went into my room to arrange my clothes, had a leisurely bath, wore a white salwar-kameez with orange sprigs and lit two candles, one for the Prophet, asking him to help me settle down, and the other for the aunt who had brought up Moses. As I looked up at her, I felt she was staring at me with a severe look. I did not know what the future held for me.

By then I was hungry. When I was heating the leftovers, the doorbell rang again. I opened the door and saw a man with a bagful of tiffin carriers. He offered me one, saying, 'Moses Saab has sent food for you.' I accepted it, wondering if Moses really cared for me. Then I told myself that it was nice of him. He had made arrangements for lunch, knowing that there was nothing in the house and I was new to Ahmedabad.

I sat at the dining table, opened the tiffin and ate a little of everything, wondering what to wear that evening. But Prophet Elijah has a solution for everything. The doorbell rang again and when I opened the door, I saw a good-looking woman standing there. She entered, introduced herself as Sippora and said that she had a beauty parlour in her apartment. As a wedding gift, she had decided to help me dress for the reception. From my saris, she helped me chose a sky-blue silk one embroidered with gold thread, with a matching blouse. She suggested that I wear the gold mangalsutra Moses had given me as a symbol of my marital status, gold bangles and gold earrings, and approved of my Kolhapuri chappals with gold straps. On the spur of the moment, she gave me an eyeliner to accentuate my eyes and asked me to wear lipstick, which she was sure I was carrying in my purse. Then she brushed my hair till it cascaded down my back.

Sippora was already dressed in a wine-red skirt and silver-spangled kurti, so she dabbed on some lipstick and sat chatting with me, as she sensed that I was tense. Moses had not returned from work and I did not know the people invited to the party. I was sitting on the edge of the sofa-chair as though I was a stranger in my own home. I jumped when I heard Moses open the door. He looked uncomfortable when he saw Sippora sitting there, smiled and disappeared into the kitchen. He ate the leftovers from the tiffin and then locked himself in his room to dress for the evening. When he emerged, he was wearing the same suit he had worn for our wedding in Alibaug, which had since been ironed. He left quickly to supervise the preparations downstairs.

Sippora accompanied me to the lawns of Shalom India Housing Society and led me to the floral dias, where Moses was already standing, giving instructions to the electrician. As soon as Sippora left me there, Moses asked me to stand next to him to greet his guests. The evening passed happily amidst flowers, lights and live music, which Franco Fernandez played on his violin, as waiters served glasses of orange juice and plates of samosas. Moses introduced me to the Jewish community of Ahmedabad, his childhood friends and office colleagues. We were given innumerable bouquets of flowers, envelopes of cash and a variety of wedding presents such as glasses, cups, wall clocks, dinner sets, cutlery and other knick-knacks, which would be useful in setting up our new home.

Then I noticed Moses watching me with a look of disapproval. I smiled and kept talking to the guests, but knew that I had displeased my husband in some way. Whatever his feelings, for appearances' sake he kept a smile pasted on his face through the evening. The reception was followed by a buffet dinner of traditional chowli or black-eyed peas, paneer in red masala curry, hot naan, spicy dal, rice, a salad and roasted papad, followed by mango ice cream.

By the end of the party, I had assumed that Moses was a gentle, quiet man, but on our way to the elevator, he hissed, 'Don't ever keep your hair open. Keep it tied.' I knew that it was going to be difficult living with a 'simple' man like Moses.

Within a week, I noticed that he had a smooth body with hardly any hair. That was his 'flaw'. While growing up, he may have wanted to have body hair like most men. Instead, his body was as hairless as a baby's bottom, so in a way, we were 'made for each other'. It was for this reason that we were not destined to make love. Maybe he hesitated because he was almost hairless. Whenever I thought about this matter, I sometimes wanted to laugh, sometimes cry ... I had neither love nor music in my life. My marriage was just a signature on a certificate.

After the wedding reception, it was understood that we would live different lives. I looked after our home and made sure that there was food on the table for my 'Lord and Master'. I accepted my fate. And whenever I spoke to my parents, I painted a rosy picture of my married life. The way I spoke, they never guessed that we slept in different rooms. When the help arrived in the morning, one of us was always up and about and my bed was always made. But I used the bathroom of the master bedroom without permission and kept my toiletries there, as a reminder to Moses that I lived in the same apartment.

Moses slept in the master bedroom, while I had made myself comfortable in the smaller bedroom, almost like a guest. The smaller bedroom is usually known as the children's room, guest room or servant's room. I arranged the room according to my needs, while the harmonium gathered dust under my bed.

When alone, I would open the harmonium and had to make an effort not to touch it. I did not play even a random note on it, for fear that one of the neighbours would hear music coming from our flat and ask Moses if I was a singer. The secret had to be buried deep within my being, even if it tormented me. I was desperate to sing a raga, but held myself back, as I had promised not to.

When Moses was at home, he often switched on the television, watched the news, a film or television serials while I held the precious iPod I had received as a gift from my childhood friends. I studied the pamphlet, learnt how to play it and listened to music with my headphones on.

Moses never came home for lunch, so it became my music hour. I lay on the sofa, reduced the volume of the television and zapped all the music channels. This life of deception went on for some time, as when Moses was not at home, I also listened to music on my iPod while doing housework, cutting vegetables, rolling chapatis and cooking.

In a way, we had drawn a line of control in our lives. We rarely spoke, but Moses had mastered the art of giving instructions about simple household matters. Maybe he had picked it up from his aunt. And, since the night of our wedding reception, I made sure that my hair was always braided or rolled into a chignon.

Every day, I heaved a sigh of relief when Moses left for work and with my iPod, I disappeared into my world of music. The sofa transformed into my flying carpet and I floated into unknown regions where Moses could never reach me.

Once in a while, I had to leave my comfort zone and accept invitations from the women of Shalom India Housing Society for a get-together, where we would talk about household matters. Gradually, this became a friendly distraction as I started opening up.

I liked Sippora. Sometimes she came to see me alone and discreetly asked if she could help me remove the unwanted hair. She knew the latest beauty treatments. She was deeply concerned and promised that she would find a solution for my allergy. These interactions helped. Otherwise life was boring and I was often depressed. But then, as they say in the Bible, 'Help comes in many ways...'

Day after day, I would stand facing the picture of Prophet Elijah and ask him to help me. Whenever I stood there, reciting the Eliayhoo Hannabi prayer, I saw the light from the window fall on his raised hand. I assumed that it would take a year or two to find a solution. I felt comforted.

Eventually, it came in the form of Matchmaker Uncle, when he was in Ahmedabad, hunting for brides and grooms as usual. Moses invited him on Friday evening for Sabbath dinner. And, being an old hand at the games men and women play, he guessed that all was not well between us. A month later, he called me to say that he had found a job for me as a music teacher in an international school on S.G. Road. It was rather far from our apartment but they had a school bus, so transportation would not be a problem. He had made an appointment for me to meet the director of the school and had even asked Sippora to drive me there. I met the lady director of the school, who saw my biodata and immediately gave me an appointment letter, asking me to join in a fortnight. I was elated.

Moreover, Matchmaker Uncle returned to Ahmedabad and came to see us and inform Moses about my new job. Moses listened, expressionless, and then, after what appeared to be ages, nodded his head in the affirmative, saying, 'Fine. If that's what Golda wants to do. In this way she can contribute to the household expenses. I always wanted a working woman as a wife. You see, my aunt worked all her life and brought me up...'

It was the beginning of a new phase for me. Life was suddenly hectic as I had to get up early and make tea, breakfast and lunch. I would leave Moses's tiffin box on the dining table, pack my own lunch, go for a shower, dress and catch the school bus, which also dropped me home in the evening. I would enter the empty apartment, heave a sigh of relief, make a leisurely cup of tea, eat a snack and go shopping to a nearby mall for vegetables and groceries. I would return to the apartment, cook dinner, set the table, pick up newspapers, clothes and empty teacups. Then, I would change into my night clothes and listen to music, waiting for Moses.

The hours I spent at school were my secret world. That was the time I recreated my world of music, far away from Moses and his silence. The school had four music rooms, two for music, two for classical Indian dance, according to the age of the students. My colleague was a well-known elderly musician who taught vocal music to senior students, while I was in charge of the junior classes. The music room was like a dream come true, as it had every possible musical instrument, arranged in glass cupboards along the walls. Suddenly, I was in a world of tunes and melodies. For a few hours, I forgot the stressful life I led with Moses. In six months, the authorities were impressed with my work. Whenever I was alone in the school music room, I would open the harmonium as though it was the most valuable object of my life and sing. I lived two lives, one silent with the iPod in the apartment, the other in school, where I had the freedom to sing.

In the school bus, on my way home, I would feel as if my songs would burst out one day and break the walls Moses had built around me, in which I felt like an imprisoned bird.

Since I had started work I had not met Sippora, so I was happy when she came over. She told me about her friend Sharon who lived in Block A and whom I had met at the wedding reception. Sharon played the sitar and was a lecturer at a local college of performing arts. Sippora sent a text message to Sharon, asking if she could join us when she returned home. She also asked me if Moses was interested in music. I did not answer. Sippora understood. I did not want Sippora and Sharon in the apartment when Moses returned so I said that I would meet Sharon some other time. I was relieved when we decided to meet at Sharon's place.

When I met Sippora and Sharon together, we bonded as though we had always known each other. Yet, I looked at Sharon's drawing room with a certain amount of envy, where her sitar was placed on a beautiful carpet, along with a pair of tablas, a tanpura and a harmonium. Sharon had the freedom to display her musical instruments in her home. Then Sharon asked me to sing. For a second I was euphoric and forgot the promise I had made to Moses. Then I told them about my problem with him. They listened compassionately and said that they wanted to help and also hear me sing. I sang for them; they liked my voice. I felt I had found another family in Ahmedabad, as we made a pact of secrecy. For the first time in months, I felt happy and loved.

Moses and I rarely spoke to each other, except regarding household matters. Sometimes he asked me to accompany him to the synagogue if there was a malida, bar mitzvah, circumcision, an engagement, a mehendi ceremony or a wedding. But I rarely got the opportunity to dress up and go to the cinema. In Alibaug, I always used to see the latest films on Saturday afternoon with my friends, after which we would have ice-cream soda at Sam Uncle's stall on the way home. Those were happy days.

Moses never suggested that we eat out at a restaurant or go to a café for coffee, samosas or ice cream. I would ask myself, 'Is this romance, love, marriage ... or am I just an extra piece of furniture in his apartment?'

But if and when Moses went to meet his office colleagues or childhood friends, I sent a text message to Sippora and Sharon. We would meet. I felt a great sense of relief spending time with them. During these secret meetings, Sippora often tried one of her beauty treatments on my arms, to see if she could solve my problem of unwanted hair, gave me a manicure, brushed my hair, taught me to braid it in different styles or gave me a facial with herbal cream, making sure it did not give me a rash. Slowly, my life was taking unpredictable turns.

A few days before the festival of Passover, Moses received a circular from Ezra that like every year, the women of the Jewish community of Ahmedabad were getting together to make matzo-bhakhris or unleavened bread, and bin-khameer-chi-bhakhri, and haroset or date-sheera at the synagogue for the community Seder. Men were also invited to make blackcurrant sherbet.

Moses read the circular aloud and, in a sarcastic, taunting voice, said, 'This is for you. You Alibaug women are used to making bhakhris ... you can go if you want to. It will remind you of your village.'

I was annoyed by his tone, for making me feel like a village girl. I controlled my temper and decided that I would go to the synagogue for the Seder preparations as an escape from him. I asked Sippora and Sharon if they would join me, but Sippora had a client and Sharon was coming later. I took leave from school and left for the synagogue. Elisheba and some other women had spread a carpet on the floor of the pavilion next to the synagogue, where they were sifting flour, making dough and rolling matzo-bhakhris. Some more women joined in as we rolled bhakhris and roasted them. I felt liberated and started humming the tune of an old Marathi kirtan about how the Patriarch Moses had led the Jews from Egypt, crossed the Red Sea with unleavened bread and received the Ten Commandments from the Lord. When Sharon arrived and saw everybody singing with me, she joined in as she began making haroset, which was her specialty. I had forgotten that I had promised Moses I would not sing in public, and was enjoying every moment with the women.

The Jewish community celebrated the Seder together. I was worried that if Moses came to know about the kirtans, there would be hell to pay.

This matter cropped up much later, during the Simha Torah, at the meeting of the executive committee of the synagogue. One of the women who had been present at the Passover preparations suggested that as I had a very good knowledge of kirtans, which were traditionally sung by Bene Israel Jews in Marathi, I should train some women, form a group and give a performance during Simha Torah. On this occasion they also had a fancy-dress competition and gave out gifts to young children. I was unaware of this, as I rarely went to the synagogue without Moses.

Weeks before Simha Torah, on Sunday, when I was making lunch, I saw Ezra enter our apartment. He spoke to Moses, who looked uncomfortable. Ezra told Moses that they had just discovered that I was a very good singer and knew Biblical kirtans in Marathi. He wanted me to teach these to the women of our community. My heartbeat increased and, although it was cold, I began to perspire profusely, worried as to what would happen when Ezra left. I knew Moses was a mouse and would not show his annoyance in Ezra's presence. But Ezra refused to leave unless I agreed to sing and called out to me, asking if I would lead the kirtan-singing programme. I stared at him, speechless, as Moses looked at me with a deadpan face and said, 'You promised that you would never sing in public.'

Ezra intervened and asked Moses, 'Did you know that your wife is a musician?'

'Yes.'

'What is wrong with you, Moses? She is an artist; you cannot kill her talent.'

'I do not like music and do not want Golda to sing in public … she is my wife…'

'Oh! yes? But she is not your slave. Let her do what she wants, like most of our women…'

Moses sat there frozen, teacup in hand, and said, 'Okay. If Golda wants to sing, who am I to stop her?'

When Ezra left, we had our first big fight. Between shouts and screams, Moses raised his hand to slap me, calling me a courtesan. I held his hand midway and shouted back at him, 'I will sing. You cannot stop me.'

That evening, with Ezra, Sippora and Sharon's help, I left for Alibaug with a few of my things and, of course, my harmonium, thanking Prophet Elijah for helping me escape.

After that, whatever happened is history.

Fortunately, before I reached Alibaug, Ezra had informed my parents that my marriage to Moses was difficult, that Moses was violent and did not respect me. This came as a shock to them. I had always painted a rosy picture of my marriage and for some reason or another, they had not come to Ahmedabad to see me, nor had I gone to Alibaug to meet them.

On reaching Alibaug, I told my parents the series of events that had occurred. I also said that just to get me married, they should not have agreed to his condition that I would never sing or practise music. This had put him in a powerful position, so much so that he did not respect me as a human being. Why he had married me was a mystery. Was it just a social obligation or a promise he had made to his aunt that he would marry a Bene Israel Jewish girl?

My old-fashioned parents were ashamed about my sudden return to Alibaug. They were uncomfortable telling relatives, friends, neighbours and the Jewish community that my marriage had not worked. But I convinced them that I could never live with Moses. In Alibaug, I went back to teaching.

Sippora and Sharon kept in touch with me. Sippora was concerned about the down on my face and arranged an appointment with a well-known dermatologist in Mumbai, who was an expert at handling delicate skin problems. Miraculously, the treatment worked, and in two years, my skin was smooth and glowing. Sippora and Sharon also gave me tips on make-up, clothes and jewellery.

Sharon sent me the phone number of a well-known vocalist in Mumbai and so, almost every weekend I was in Mumbai, either for skincare or training with the vocalist. I was transforming from an ugly duckling into a swan.

My music teacher in Mumbai was sure that I was made for greater things in life and promoted me at various concerts. By then, I had asked for a divorce from Moses, which was granted and I was free to follow my dreams.

But this is not the end of the story.

Salome told Sippora, and eventually me, that on a certain Sunday evening, when Moses was zapping channels on TV, he saw me dressed in a colourful nine-yard Maharashtrian sari singing a folk song with gusto, which was judged as the best performance at a reality show. I am sure Moses was shocked when my name was announced as the best singer of the season.

Overnight, I became India's singing star. I often mixed Hindi, English, Hebrew and Marathi words in my songs. I was invited to a concert of Indian music in Israel and acclaimed as a 'Jewish Nightingale'. My photographs were splashed in the media and Jewish newsletters all over the world.

Sippora and Sharon informed me that soon afterwards, Moses disappeared from Shalom India Housing Society and was never seen again, although Salome was sure that he was in Ahmedabad.

I had realized my dreams and was floating on my flying carpet among the stars…

12

Ilana

ILANA HAD TRAINED as a police officer. Since then, she had decided that Jewish suitors were not for her. She felt that she was stronger than most men. Whenever she agreed to meet a suitor to respect her parents' feelings, she was certain that he would not be good enough for her.

With hard work, Ilana had risen to the post of deputy superintendent of police and wanted a husband to match her education and status. Being a policewoman was part of her family tradition. She had grown up listening to stories of her powerful grandmother Sara, who had been the superintendent of Sabarmati Jail. She had been honoured with the President's Medal for prison reforms. And Aunt Rose held pride of place in the family, as she had trained as a policewoman in Israel after she lost her husband in a shootout. With such a background, Ilana was looking for a person who could stand shoulder to shoulder with her in the long journey of life. She was doubly careful, as she did not want to be burdened with a man who did not respect her achievements.

Past thirty, she lived a busy but uneventful life with her parents Noah and Leah in A-105 at Shalom India Housing Society. Like her grandmother Sara, she loved to dress up in her uniform and feel powerful. She had a room to herself in her parents' home. A police jeep was at her disposal, which she never used for personal work, only official duties.

Ilana's life changed when she received a marriage proposal from Amos. He was Salome's nephew from Mumbai. He was also a police officer and that was the reason Salome had suggested he meet Ilana. Leah prayed to Prophet Elijah that he play the matchmaker for her beautiful but hot-headed daughter.

Although they were both police officers, Amos was fun-loving and different from Ilana. So Salome had her doubts that they would get along. Ilana never smiled, unless there was a good reason. She was tall, well built, had a square jaw, large black eyes, a small mouth and short hair. Salome had convinced Ilana's parents that Amos was the perfect match for her. He had the same post as Ilana in Mumbai, and he was also tall and lean and had a pleasant round face.

Amos came from Mumbai to meet Ilana. He was staying with Salome, who had informed Noah and Leah about his arrival. So they invited him for tea when Ilana returned from work. They had informed her about the proposal and she had agreed to meet him to please her parents and Aunt Salome, whom she liked because she was simple, large-hearted and had been close to grandmother Sara.

That evening, when Ilana and Amos were introduced, she did not particularly like him. But after Leah had served tea and biscuits, she suggested that they go out to a café. Ilana agreed, as she did not want to sit opposite Amos and her own family all evening. During the outing, she was sure to put him off and refuse the marriage proposal. To gain time, she excused herself, went to her room, took off her uniform, and folded and put it away. She carefully dressed up in a bright pink kurta over black tights, combed her hair in an upward sweep, applied eyeliner, wore brown lipstick and dabbed her favourite perfume behind her ears. When she came out Amos smiled, pointed at her photograph in uniform kept on the mantelpiece and asked, 'Are you the same person?' She smiled back enigmatically.

They took an autorickshaw from the gates of Shalom India Housing Society. Ilana gave instructions to the driver. The coffee shop was far, but she assured Amos that it was cosy. Halfway, before they had reached the café, Amos suddenly felt hungry. It was past 6 in the evening but not really dinnertime. Ilana did not remind him that he had just eaten biscuits at her place. She started having doubts about getting married to a man for whom she would have to keep a well-stocked kitchen. She wanted to reject him immediately and return home in that very auto. But she decided to go through with the evening, as Amos was sitting at the edge of the seat of the auto, enjoying the sights of Ahmedabad. She decided to give him a chance. She asked him if he was really hungry or just joking. He nodded. 'I would like to eat something spicy.' As the autorickshaw raced through the university area, he spotted a falafel van and asked, 'Can we have falafel?'

'It is not Israeli falafel, but Gujarati.'

'That's fine with me.'

So they stopped, paid the auto, stood there and ate falafel. It was just a wrap with a filling of vegetables and hummus, but he liked it. He also made a pact with Ilana that he would pay the autorickshaw fare and for whatever he ate that evening. Ilana was amused and asked if they could go ahead and have coffee. He agreed. So they took another auto and went on towards the café. There, Amos chose to sit at a road-facing glass window and ordered cappuccino for himself, while Ilana decided to have green tea. She got the feeling that he was not particularly interested in her. She assumed that maybe he too was going through the evening just to please his aunt. They sat there for almost an hour, chatting about their work, when he suddenly changed the topic and asked, 'What sort of cakes do they have here?'

'They have ordinary cakes. Are you hungry again?'

'Yes.'

Ilana was relieved. She assumed that the alliance would not come through—Amos was only interested in food, not her. They laughed and joked like old friends. There was nothing romantic about their outing, but they were enjoying themselves.

Amos's mood was infectious and Ilana offered to take him to a restaurant where they served the best dark chocolate cakes. She hesitated, as it was getting late and the restaurant was far away, but Amos was game as long as he could have cake. They stopped another auto, but when they were on their way to the cake shop, Amos noticed a Lebanese restaurant and insisted that they stop there and try out a real falafel. Ilana was feeling as exhilarated as Amos and agreed to stop at the restaurant, joking, 'Okay, let us say this is a dinner date of sorts.'

The falafel was better than the roadside one and for the first time in the evening, they talked about their likes and dislikes. This conversation made Ilana uncomfortable but Amos smiled broadly, and to put her at ease, said, 'You are fun.'

Ilana's face tightened. She replied, 'I am not. I am a very serious police officer. Now shall we go home?'

Amos immediately became cautious, stood up, saluted her as though he was her subordinate and apologized. 'Sorry, officer, I rarely have time to go out or enjoy myself. As you wish, madam, I am ready to go back.'

Ilana realized that she had punctured his mood and feeling annoyed with herself, suddenly smiled graciously. She decided to end the evening on a pleasant note and asked, 'Now what else would you like to eat, Mr Officer?'

'How about that special chocolate cake, please?'

Like two giddy teenagers, they found one more auto. When they reached the cake shop, she ordered one huge chocolate pastry known as 'Hot Lava'. With two spoons and the pastry, dripping with hot chocolate sauce, placed between them, they ate, laughed and talked about everything but the marriage proposal.

It was almost midnight when they returned, as they had had to walk a long distance to find another autorickshaw. At the gates of Shalom India Housing Society, they stopped laughing, as Ilana wanted to maintain her strict demeanour. She nodded, gave him a tight smile and went to the elevator which took her to A-105 while Amos rang the doorbell of Aunt Salome's apartment on the ground floor.

Next morning, when Leah asked Ilana if she would consider Amos as a prospective groom, as he was leaving for Mumbai that evening, Ilana nodded her head in the affirmative, as though it was the most natural thing on earth. Amos smiled when he was told this. He knew he could never have convinced Ilana to accept his proposal had he not taken her café-hopping. That night, Ilana had fallen in love with Amos.

When Leah informed Salome about Ilana's decision, Amos came over to Ilana's house, smiled and saluted his fiancée with a twinkle in his eyes. Salome rushed down to her apartment and lit a candle for Prophet Elijah, as he smiled down at her.

13

Flora

The Big Fat Jewish Wedding

T HEY SAY MARRIAGES are made in heaven, but for Joseph and Flora, theirs was made on earth. The bride and groom were plump, in their late thirties, had never received a marriage proposal and faced the possibility of 'missing the boat'.

Flora lived in Ahmedabad and ran a playgroup for pre-schoolers at home. Friends, relatives and neighbours often commented that she loved children and had she married, she would have made an excellent mother. Joseph, a Jewish banker from Mumbai, had been brought up by his maternal aunt, as he had lost his parents early in life. With his aunt's growing family, he often felt like an outsider and decided to live on his own. He asked the head office of his bank for a transfer to Gujarat. That is how he came to Bhuj and then to Ahmedabad after a promotion. Joseph was pleased as his distant uncle Samuel lived there in an upmarket satellite area, in Shalom

135

India Housing Society. Jews lived in Block A of the society while other communities were allotted Block B.

Like some others in this narrative, Flora and Joseph were not residents of Shalom India Housing Society. Flora's aunt Sippora also lived there so Joseph and Flora were often there to meet their respective relatives. Maybe, before they were introduced, they took the same elevator to go up to apartments A-103 and A-112, not knowing what the future held for them.

On arrival, Joseph had stayed as a paying guest with his bank manager's brother. Then he came down with a stomach infection and had to be admitted to a private hospital near Shalom India Housing Society, so that Samuel could look after him. It had not been easy for Samuel as his wife Sharon, a musician, taught sitar at a private college of performing arts and did not have much time to look after Joseph.

When Joseph was discharged from the hospital, Samuel decided that he should stay with them. Sharon liked him, as he was not demanding, managed well on his own and, above all, was non-intrusive. When he was better, she suggested that he rent Juliet and Romiel's apartment A-107. It was vacant since their last tenant Lisa, who had been interning with an NGO, had returned to Zurich.

Joseph saw the apartment with its bare necessities and, as a Bene Israel Jew, felt blessed when he noticed a poster of Prophet Elijah on the wall. He readily agreed to rent it, as he could be independent and yet be close to family. As a follow-up, Samuel spoke to Ezra, the president and builder of Shalom India Housing Society, who wrote an email to Juliet about renting her flat to Joseph. He wrote that Joseph was a nice young man who was willing to give the deposit and regularly transfer the rent in her bank account. Juliet agreed.

When the papers were signed and the advance rent deposited, Joseph shifted to A-107 with his meagre belongings. He had a bed, a cupboard, a work table, a coffee table which was also his dining table, a television set, two chairs, his mother's rocking chair, a small refrigerator, a hot plate and a box of pots, pans and crockery. Samuel also asked the young boy who worked for Franco Fernandez in Block B to clean Joseph's apartment, wash dishes, take his clothes to the dhobi and run errands.

Although Sharon offered to send him food in the evenings, Joseph politely refused. He would have lunch in the office canteen and dinner at a thali restaurant nearby or he would order a pizza on his way home. Sharon was impressed that his refrigerator was always stocked with bread, butter, eggs, cheese, fruit, cartons of milk and yoghurt, so that when he was hard-pressed for time, he could make sandwiches, an omelette and a glass of hot chocolate milk. Sharon often invited him for Sabbath dinner or Sunday lunch.

Flora lived in East Ahmedabad in the opposite direction to Shalom India Housing Society, but was often at Sippora's place. She was fond of Sippora's children, and also gave them tuitions. She sometimes stayed over if Sippora and Opher were invited out for dinner or went for a late-night movie.

As destiny would have it, on a certain Saturday afternoon, when they were on their way back from Sharon's nephew Reuben's bar mitzvah at the synagogue, Sippora's son was fast asleep in Flora's lap, so Joseph offered to carry him to the lift. When they were all standing at Sippora's door, Prophet Elijah planted the thought in Sippora's romantic mind that maybe Joseph and Flora were made for each other. Quickly, she invited the whole group for coffee at her place. They agreed. When the coffee was ready, the women carried the cups and plates of biscuits to the drawing room. While offering coffee to Joseph, Flora felt strangely drawn to him, as he had a friendly smile. Till then he had not noticed her, except that she looked kind and had sparkling eyes.

Later, Sippora asked Sharon, 'Is Joseph married?'

'Why are you interested in Fatty?'

'Just like that...'

'Come on, Sippora, you never ask a question without a reason. Don't tell me you find him attractive because he has a big paunch. You like them with their six-pack abs and broad chests...'

'Well, he is rather on the round side, but there is something about him. He looks like a good human being.'

'Yes, he is a nice young man. He is still unmarried because he is fat. Most girls reject him as soon as they see his paunch. So we stopped matchmaking for him.'

Sippora gave her a sunny smile and said, 'You know, marriages are made in heaven, but this one is going to be made in Shalom India Housing Society.'

'What do you mean? I don't see a suitable bride for Joseph.'

'Don't worry, I have chosen one for him.'

'What do you mean? How?'

'Well, Flora is the perfect match for Joseph.'

'Come on, Sippora. She is really fat. Have you seen the tyres around her waist?'

'Okay, if Flora is fat, what is Joseph? Amitabh Bachchan?'

Sharon was embarrassed. 'Yes, he is on the heavy side. But whenever I have spoken to him about marriage and asked him about the sort of girl he would like to marry, he's laughed and said that he is looking for someone petite. You know, as they say, opposites attract. If you ask Flora, she would tell you that she likes them tall, dark and handsome. So I don't think it will work. Whatever the size, we human beings have our fantasies.'

Not to be defeated, Sippora sat cross-legged on the floor and mused, 'Well, whatever our dreams, at some point in life, we all make compromises. Let them meet and decide.'

'Listen, Sippora, if your romantic ideas don't work and one of them refuses, I am afraid our relationship will be strained forever...'

'We don't have to make a formal proposal. We can just get them together, like today. Both of us can plan meetings here or at the synagogue. Then we can leave it to Prophet Elijah to play matchmaker.'

'In Juliet's flat, the Prophet sometimes plays matchmaker, but not always. Let us hope for the best.'

'Exactly...'

'But it has to be our secret.'

'Done...'

Soon after, both women made every effort to get Joseph and Flora together and decided to follow the famous saying, 'The way to a man's heart is through his stomach.'

As part of Operation Matchmaking, Sippora and Sharon planned a Sunday lunch and invited Joseph. He readily agreed. It was easy for Sippora to rope in Flora, as Flora tutored her daughters on Saturday afternoons, helped them with their homework and, before leaving, took them downstairs to play a game of badminton. Sippora's youngest was not yet four and was often at Salome's, as she looked after him when Sippora was busy. The girls loved Flora. So, on a certain Saturday, a day before the luncheon, Sippora left the children with Flora and went shopping. On her return, she asked Flora to help her sort the vegetables, marinate the fish and freeze it. When the kitchen was organized, Sippora feigned a headache and Flora made coffee for her and asked her to rest. She helped the children wash, change and even fed them. She then herded them into their room, returned to Sippora and said, 'If you are feeling better I will go home, as it is getting dark.'

'I am not feeling well. Could you stay back tonight and help me tomorrow morning? If you agree, I will call your mother.'

'Don't worry, I will call Mamma.'

Sippora wanted Flora to cook. She had planned that halfway through the next day's lunch, she would announce that Flora was the chef, so that Joseph would be impressed by her and overlook her weight. And, as part of her act, hand on forehead, she told Flora that

Sharon was bringing rice and vegetables, but refrained from adding that Joseph was also invited.

Sippora invited Flora to the lunch. At first she hesitated, as she had not brought a change of clothes. Affectionately, Sippora brushed aside her concerns, saying they would work it out. But Flora insisted that she would wake up early, help her cook, return home, change and come back for the party. Sippora kept quiet, as she had other plans. In the past, whenever Sippora was unwell, Flora had stayed back to help. The children were excited that Flora would be spending the night in their bedroom, as she would allow them to read and play computer games.

Sippora gave a nightdress to Flora and suggested that she have an early dinner and retire, as they had a long day ahead. Next morning, Sippora woke up, inhaling the aromatic flavours emitting from the kitchen. Coffee mug in hand and dressing gown flapping around her shapely legs, she tossed the salad. Flora told her to relax, as she preferred to work alone in the kitchen. So Sippora set the table and instructed the maid to clean the apartment. By then, Flora had made the fish curry.

Flora was now feeling sweaty in the kitchen. She decided not to stay for lunch, as she needed a shower, a change of clothes and had promised her neighbour's children that she would help them prepare for their forthcoming exams. It would be too much of a bother to go home and return for the party. But Sippora was adamant that she stay on and wear one of her salwar-kameezes. She showed her a mauve dress, which her Aunt Leora from Israel had left behind when she had come to meet her. Flora liked its embroidered borders, elbow-length sleeves and stylish parallel pants. The short scarf was of the same colour. Sippora knew that mauve was Flora's favourite colour and the dress would fit her perfectly. Flora went for a shower and emerged from the children's room, looking fresh, trim and attractive.

Sippora was impressed to see Flora looking chic; she usually appeared dowdy in misshapen clothes. She persuaded her to wear lipstick and apply kohl on her eyes. Flora looked at herself in the dressing-room mirror and felt good. She did not protest when Sippora brushed her hair and urged her to leave it loose, saying, 'Flora, you must always dress like this.'

'Why?'

'For yourself!'

'But, I feel overdressed, as though I am going to a wedding.'

'Maybe you are…'

'What?'

'Just joking.'

Before the others arrived, Sippora put on an indigo-blue skirt with a grey T-shirt and surprised Flora by applying a touch of perfume behind her ears. Flora breathed in the fragrance and giggled. 'What is it?'

'Rose of Sharon…'

Sippora left the apartment door open as Sharon, Samuel and their children trooped in, carrying casseroles of food. Sharon was pleased to see Flora in her new avatar as they carried the food into the kitchen. Sippora welcomed Joseph, who was awkwardly standing at the door with a carton of mango ice cream for dessert.

When they had settled down in the drawing room, Sippora offered them glasses of orange juice, but her heart sank when she saw that Joseph and Flora did not seem particularly interested in talking. Though they shook hands, they did not seem to notice each other; the men discussed cricket while Flora played cards with the children and kept them busy.

It was the same during dinner, but almost at the end of the meal, Joseph asked for another helping. Sippora and Sharon were surprised when he was all praise for the fish curry, saying that it was made exactly the way his mother used to. Quickly, Sippora gave the credit to Flora. Later, Joseph helped Flora serve the ice cream and they started chatting. Sippora and Sharon smiled as though they had won a battle.

When the table was cleared, Joseph and Flora moved to the balcony and leaning over the parapet, continued their conversation. The children ran around them, demanding that Flora play with them till Sippora shooed them away, insisting that they take a nap.

Joseph told Flora that the fish curry had reminded him of his childhood and made him nostalgic for his mother's cooking. She was touched when he told her about his childhood in Mumbai. Joseph rarely spoke about his mother, but that day told Flora that she was an excellent homemaker who ran the house on minimum finances, as his father's income as a railway booking clerk was not enough to make ends meet. She was well known for her knowledge of Jewish recipes. She preferred only to cook for the family, but once in a while during festivals, she would cater for some Jewish families. She became a reluctant caterer when her husband died of a heart attack. But before she could organize her business, she too died of a lung infection, which she had neglected. Flora saw that his eyes were wet and changed the subject, asking, 'How do you manage alone?'

'It's easy. I almost always eat at the office canteen and, if I am very hungry, I order pizza. I always have eggs in the fridge at home and sometimes pick up something on the way back. But sometimes I do crave fish curry…'

'In that case, you must meet my mother. She is a superb cook.' Right then, her cell phone rang and smiling, she whispered, 'It's Mamma.'

She spoke to her mother, cut the call and like an obedient daughter, excused herself, saying she had to rush home. She returned to the drawing room, shook hands with everybody and said, 'I must leave, Mamma is all worked up.' She ran to the children's room to get her bag, returned and, standing in the doorway, told Sippora that she would return the dress the next week. Then Joseph came forward and asked her if she had a scooter.

'No,' replied Flora, smiling. 'I will find an autorickshaw. It takes me forty minutes to reach home.' Joseph gallantly offered to drop her on his scooter. Flora agreed rather hesitantly, saying, 'Sure, I would like you to meet Mamma.' Joseph asked her to wait downstairs, thanked the others and left to get his scooter keys.

That was the beginning of Joseph and Flora's friendship. Sippora and Sharon waited for them to fall in love. They noted that their weight did not stop them from being friends. Maybe it was a matter of time before they decided to get married.

By then, both women had told Opher and Samuel about the possibility of a wedding in the family. The men were sceptical, but not the women as they schemed to get them together on every possible occasion.

Then one evening on his way back from work, Opher saw Flora and Joseph at a café, laughing over coffee and cakes. That night he told Sippora, 'If the two heavyweights are not worried about their calories, they should not have any problem in getting married.' So, instead of two heads, four heads got together to get Joseph and Flora married.

Soon after, one afternoon when Flora was at Sippora's, she invited Flora for lunch. While heaping her plate with rice and dal, she asked, 'Would you consider Joseph as a possible groom?'

Stunned, Flora asked, 'For whom?'

'You.'

Flora burst out laughing. 'Do you think he would like to get married to me?'

Sippora hugged her. 'Why not? You are a darling.'

'Well yes … I would … if … he …' Flora was blushing.

Immediately, Sippora sent a text message to Sharon and gave her the good news.

Meanwhile, during his lunch break, Samuel invited Joseph to a Chinese restaurant and told him point-blank, 'Joseph, now that you are well settled, I advise you to get married.'

'Come on, Samuel, look at me. No girl in her right mind would want to marry me.'

By then, Samuel had received Sharon's text message that Flora had agreed to marry Joseph, so he said, 'I think Flora would make the perfect wife for you.'

Much to his surprise, Joseph smiled. 'Are you joking? I really like her. But would she … ?'

'Sure,' said Samuel and showed him Sharon's message.

Joseph appeared rather nervous as he mumbled, 'I like her very much.'

Soon, in keeping with Jewish tradition, as Samuel was related to Joseph, he sent a formal marriage proposal to Flora's parents, asking for their daughter's hand. They accepted immediately. This was the beginning of preparations for the Big Fat Jewish Wedding.

Flora did not know what she was in for when Sippora and Sharon started planning her trousseau, rituals, ceremonies, reception, invitation card and other details. She knew how extravagant they could be and gave them a budget, which was approved by her father. But caution bells started ringing when they insisted that she had to lose weight for the wedding photograph.

Flora refused, saying stubbornly, 'Joseph likes me the way I am. Why don't you ask him to lose weight?'

'It is different for men. But for a bride, it is her right to look beautiful on her wedding day.'

'I will think about it.'

A week later, Flora informed them that she could not go through with the slimming programme, as she was running short of money. Not to be deterred, Sippora and Salome offered to help by putting her on a strict diet and teaching her exercises which could be done at home. Sippora started working on Flora at her beauty parlour, applying creams, giving massages, pedicures and manicures. Soon, like all brides, Flora started fantasizing about how beautiful she would look on her wedding day.

However, when 'Project Beauty' started taking up all her time, Flora thought of abandoning it, as she was having to cancel her tutoring assignments. Besides, she could hardly spend any time with Joseph. He understood her plight and explained that maybe she would not regret it when she looked radiant on their wedding day. He did not want to hurt her by telling her that he also wanted her to lose weight for the wedding reception, when she would be under the scrutiny of their guests.

But he felt guilty about persuading her to join Sippora's regime, especially when he saw himself in the bathroom mirror and realized that he also needed to lose weight. But as a man, he did not have to face the same pressure as Flora. Besides, he did not have time to join a gymnasium, as he was working overtime to take a few days' leave for the wedding festivities and maybe a short honeymoon somewhere … he was not sure where.

Flora went through long hours of workouts, which made her joints ache. It was hard for her to live on small quantities of food four times a day, minus rice, oil, ghee, butter, snacks and chocolates. Sippora had given a list of permissible foods to Flora's mother, who was convinced that this was the best way for her daughter to lose weight. Even when Flora craved for chocolates, she stopped herself by thinking of her dream wedding photograph.

A month before the wedding, Sippora was happy with her handiwork. Flora still looked plump, but attractive in a voluptuous way, as some bulges were in the right places.

But Flora's torture did not end. The strict regime was to last another month and a half. Sharon was in charge of Flora's wardrobe and when the fittings started, Flora had to squeeze into the clothes, which were a size smaller than what she usually wore. She had to hold her breath, so much so that she almost decided not to get married and called Joseph to meet her at a café.

She reached before him and waited, having ordered chocolate cake, which she ate with a look of disgust writ large on her face. Joseph joined her, took a spoonful and complimented her on her new look. He was taken aback when she started sobbing. She wiped her tears and said, 'I hate it. I cannot enjoy anything. I feel suffocated with all this slimming, dieting and dress rehearsals. I really cannot go through with this. Sorry, Joseph, I cannot get married. I was so happy when I was fat; at least I was myself…' All Joseph could do was hold her hand. He was stunned by her outburst and worried that Flora had really decided to call off the wedding. A practical man, he was thinking about the invitation cards and the wedding reception hall they had booked. Besides, his wedding suit had cost a fortune, as also the fancy sherwani Sharon had forced him to buy for the mehendi ceremony. He felt disgusted with himself that instead of being concerned about Flora's anguish, he was worried about finances. He offered her another spoonful of cake. 'Have some. It is good for both of us…'

She wiped her tears and said, 'I feel horrible with so many dos and don'ts. I am tired and want to live like before. I was happy being fat, with not a worry in the world. I was a free bird. I cannot go through with this wedding, with so many restrictions.'

'Have I forced you to lose weight? I like you the way you are. But if you don't want to go through the wedding now, I can wait. We can have a long engagement. I will inform everybody that we have decided to postpone our wedding. Flora, I don't want to lose you. I love you. But let me tell you, after all the torture you have gone through, you look beautiful.'

'If I stop dieting, I may not be able to get into the wedding gown. It is tailored to my present measurements. Do you really mean it—I look nice?'

'Gorgeous.'

Flora beamed and asked him about his guest list, as she was in charge of arranging accommodation for guests from Mumbai. She had booked the synagogue guest house and a small hotel nearby, to make it easy for them to reach the venue. When they had finished discussing these details, it was time for Flora to return for a fitting, so Joseph paid the bill and asked, 'Are we still getting married?'

'Yes.'

Holding her hand, he looked deep into her eyes and said, 'I love you.'

Flora slowly came to terms with her slimmer silhouette and glowing complexion. She would often try on a new dress and study the contours of her figure in the mirror and was satisfied with what she saw.

The grand day arrived.

After the mehendi ceremony and wedding, Flora and Joseph left for Udaipur, as Sippora and Sharon had gifted them a honeymoon package of three nights and four days at a palace resort. On their return, they made a little love-nest for themselves in A-107 at Shalom India Housing Society.

During this period, they looked at the wedding photographs on Joseph's laptop together. Everybody complimented Flora for looking like a bride form a wedding-dress manual. In response, Flora told them that Joseph had surprised her when he had lifted her veil. His salt-and-pepper hair had been dyed a deep black. For a second she thought she was marrying the wrong man! Joseph guffawed and told Shwon and Sippora, 'I decided to dye my hair, as both of you had ganged up to make Flora look like a beauty queen. So I decided to look like a king.'

Joseph and Flora started looking for an apartment nearby. They even sent an email to Juliet, offering to buy A-107, which had determined their destiny. Juliet refused, as she was sentimental about the apartment and maybe later, she and Romiel would return to India and settle down in Ahmedabad.

Flora's life became hectic. She rushed between household chores, shopping, cooking, tuitions and searching for an apartment. She lost a little more weight, while Joseph remained the same.

Enthused by her trim figure, Flora became conscious of her looks and dressed with care. In her fat phase, she would stitch her own clothes, as she felt awkward giving measurements to the local tailor or trying on clothes at a boutique, for fear that the salesgirls would make fun of her. In her new avatar, she bought clothes from a boutique, which had free-size clothes that accentuated her contours. But, to Joseph's embarrassment, she had almost given up wearing a dupatta. Instead, she wore scarves around her shoulders, as she was no longer ashamed of her bust. Joseph reluctantly complimented her as his eyes rested on her beautiful bosom and moved away. He was annoyed that other men also noticed her.

He became aware that Flora could no longer be termed fat. But he forgot about it temporarily when they found a two-bedroom apartment and moved into their new home. It was in a high-rise condominium, Liberty Apartments, and they chose their lucky number 107 on the seventh floor. They moved in with a double bed, some racks, a round dining table, a few chairs and Joseph's old furniture, including the rocking chair, which fitted perfectly into the drawing room. Besides these, they had received innumerable wedding gifts like bedsheets, casseroles, tea sets, crockery, wall clocks and some knick-knacks. Samuel–Sharon and Flora's parents had gifted them cupboards and kitchen racks, while Sippora–Opher had given them curtains of their choice.

One day, Joseph returned home early to help Flora organize the flat before they had the traditional Eliyahu Hanavi prayers, malida and dinner to affix a mezuzah on their doorpost.

When he opened the door, he thought he had entered the wrong apartment. He could not recognize Flora—she was in shorts and a T-shirt, with her hair piled on her head. Wordlessly he closed the door and helped her shift the furniture in the drawing room. Flora was unaware of Joseph's discomfort as the maid arrived to help. That was when Joseph casually asked her, 'Aren't you going to change?'

She looked up, surprised. 'Why? I can work better in these clothes.' He would have preferred that she was fully covered in a salwar-kameez when the maid arrived, but chose to keep silent. Then his eyes fell on her dainty feet. He had always admired her feet. Suddenly, he was aroused and held her in his arms passionately. At first she resisted on the pretext of cleaning the house, but then gave in. He closed the bedroom door and they made love on the floor. Later, after giving him a passionate kiss, Flora dressed and went back to cleaning the house. Joseph locked himself in the bathroom and stood stark naked in front of the mirror, feeling embarrassed at his flab. That very evening Joseph joined a gym to lose weight. He wanted to be the perfect match for Flora.

That was the beginning of a long story…

In less than a year, Joseph lost a lot of weight. His clothes started hanging on him. Sippora flung into action and persuaded him to buy new clothes. He had worn standard cuts all his life, so Sippora, Sharon and Flora went shopping with him to the best menswear store in Ahmedabad. After a lot of choosing, discarding and trying on the latest styles, Joseph surprised them by buying an assortment of well-fitting jeans and the best branded T-shirts in dark colours, along with some formal shirts for high-power meetings. On the spur of the moment, he also bought a grey designer suit. He decided to give away his old clothes to a charity, so that he was not tempted to wear them again.

In the matter of slimming, Joseph had fared better than Flora. Even after losing weight, she looked a little plump. Joseph, on the other hand, had a sleek, lean look and his high cheekbones were suddenly visible. The new Joseph looked handsome and together they were a good-looking couple. In fact, whenever they were together at the synagogue or at Shalom India Housing Society, the conversation revolved around them.

Joseph and Flora had a set lifestyle with a fixed timetable. Five days a week, Joseph went to work from 10 a.m. to 6 p.m. with his lunch box, which Flora prepared while making breakfast. As a rule, when he set off, she stood on their balcony watching him as he wiped his scooter and wore his helmet. They waved before he left. Then Flora finished her household chores, bathed, dressed, had lunch while watching television, napped on the sofa, set her cellphone alarm for 2 p.m., woke up, washed her face and waited for the first batch of schoolchildren to troop in for their class. The second batch arrived at 4 p.m. and left at 6. Later, she went shopping to a nearby mall and by the time she returned home, Joseph was back.

They had dinner by 8 p. m., then Joseph went down for a stroll in the society garden and Flora watched her favourite television show till he returned to watch the late-night news, after which they went to bed. On weekends they took it easy, went to the gym together, had a late lunch, napped, shopped at the mall or went to the cinema. Sometimes on Friday evenings, they went to the synagogue for Sabbath prayers. They also made it a point to attend any bar mitzvah or circumcision ceremony on Saturday mornings.

For Sunday lunch they joined Sippora, Sharon and their families and had potluck in one house or the other. They understood the meaning of being happily married.

Then everything changed. Joseph received a promotion and had no time for Flora, so she increased the hours of her tuition classes. This worked for a while, as she was always busy and did not bother Joseph about not spending time with her.

Soon, their blissful cloud nine existence had a black lining. All hell broke loose one day when Joseph, who went to the gym early in the morning, returned late and forgot his cell phone on the dining table. Flora was in the kitchen when she heard the insistent ringing of the phone and, assuming it was an urgent call from his office, rushed to pick it up so that she could give it to him, as he was in the shower. That was when she noticed a name flashing on the screen with the image of the caller.

It was a woman with raven-black hair and bright red lipstick...

Suspicious, Flora put the phone back on the dining table and returned to the kitchen to pack Joseph's lunch box, which she was sure he never ate but emptied in the garbage bin on his way home. Of course, he had other lunches, maybe with Vishakha. That was the name which had flashed on the cell phone.

Joseph also heard his phone ringing and rushed out of the bathroom, towel tied around his waist, dripping wet, to pick up the call. He saw Flora standing in the kitchen doorway, hand on hip. She thundered, 'Who is she?'

Joseph glared back at her and growled, 'New trainer at the gym. An old friend from Mumbai,' and went back inside, slamming the bathroom door. That was the beginning of their war.

That afternoon Flora called Sippora and, not knowing what to say, fumbled for words. 'You know Joseph looks very handsome these days...'

'Yes, what's new...'

'He looks incredible. He has six-pack abs and thinks he looks like Shah Rukh Khan.'

'What are you trying to tell me?'

'You know how many kilos he has lost?'

'I remember. Has he lost some more?'

'Yes, he looks great.'

'Good for him.'

'Now that he has less time, he goes to the gym early in the morning.'

'How about you?'

'I don't work out anymore.'

'Have you put on weight?'

'A little.'

'You must be careful, or else…'

'I am okay.'

'How much have you gained?'

'Just a little, but I am stable.'

'Why have you put on weight? I thought you went to the gym on weekends. Now that you have more time, why don't you work out every day? Go to the gym with Joseph.'

'Doctor advised me not to…'

'Why?'

'I think … I am pregnant.'

'What do you mean, think? Either you are pregnant or not … Why didn't you tell us?'

'I am in a bad mood.'

'It happens during the first few months. Tell me, how many months?'

'Almost three.'

'When did you come to know?'

'Yesterday.'

'Mazal tov! Joseph must be excited?'

'He does not know.'

'Why haven't you told him?'

'Just like that.'

'Flora, I know you so well. You never hide anything from Joseph and this is great news.'

'I did not feel like telling him.'

'I don't believe it. Is something wrong? Have you had a fight?'

'...'

'Flora, are you there?'

'Yes.'

'Well, I sense something is wrong. I am coming to your place right away.'

'Okay.'

Sippora quickly cancelled all appointments, took the lift to the basement and drove to Flora's place. In this particular matter, she did not want to involve Sharon, as it concerned the family. After all, they were Joseph's relatives and this was a serious issue, as Flora had hidden such important information from Joseph.

When Sippora reached the apartment, she saw that the door was open, so she rushed in slamming the door behind her. Flora was slumped on the sofa, zapping television channels. Sippora sat next to her, held her in her arms and asked, 'What happened?'

Between sobs, Flora told her about the early-morning call and the change in Joseph since he had become regional manager of the bank. Then Sippora made coffee for both of them and advised her not to take such things seriously. She told her how someone had spread the rumour that she was having an affair with Raphael, but it was not true. Before Sippora left, Flora promised that she would give Joseph the good news that very evening. The older woman also advised her to look beautiful, not a frump. Flora gave her a weak smile.

After Sippora left, Flora called Joseph and asked him to meet her at a café. She dressed carefully, wearing a printed red skirt, a tunic of the same colour, a scarf to match and left her hair flowing over her shoulders. They had decided to meet around 4, when Joseph was not hard-pressed for time. Flora looked at her wristwatch and saw that he was late. Twice, she sent back the waiter, saying that she was waiting for someone and sat there with a sinking heart, looking out of the glass window. Then she saw him and waved. He came in hurriedly, apologizing that he had been caught in a traffic jam. Yes, the car was a new addition in their life.

Flora gave him a forced smile as he ordered two cappuccinos and a slice of truffle cake with two spoons, just as in the good old days, behaving as though nothing had happened that morning. Flora changed the order and asked for green tea. Joseph looked surprised. 'Since when did you start having green tea?'

'About two months ago. I am pregnant.'

Flora noticed that Joseph froze in his chair, as though they were playing a game of 'Statue'. She felt that he was more shocked than taken aback, more worried than happy. She sat there, expressionless and feeling miserable. She had expected him to jump with joy, pick her up in his arms, swing her around, kiss her and announce to the world, 'Look, guys, I am going to become a daddy.'

Nothing like that happened. Fortunately, at that moment the waiter arrived with the coffee, tea and cake. Joseph sat looking at the heart-shaped froth in his cup, broke it with his teaspoon and offered the cake to Flora with a tight smile. 'Great news, let us celebrate.'

Flora refused, saying, 'I don't like cakes.'

'One of those pregnancy things…'

She did not answer. She looked into his eyes and said, 'Don't lie, Joseph. I can see you are not happy with the news.'

Looking sheepish, he said, 'Naturally, it comes as a surprise. We were careful, no? We had decided to plan the baby. I did not even know that you had been to a gynaecologist. When did you come to know?'

'When could I have told you? I barely see you. We don't eat together or spend time together. This morning, when I was about to give you the good news, your phone rang.'

He was amused. 'Are you upset about Vishakha? She is a school friend from Mumbai. I can call her home for tea on a Sunday. You can meet her. It's nothing. I am so happy that we are going to be parents.'

Flora sat there trying to hold back her tears. But Joseph had paid the bill and was on his way out. He said, 'Come, let's go. I'll drop you home. I am getting late.' Flora stood up and noticed that the cake was untouched. She wanted to throw up.

Back home, she called Sippora and told her about Joseph's reaction when she told him about her pregnancy. He had made an effort to look happy. She also told her that maybe there was nothing between him and Vishakha.

As her pregnancy progressed, Flora was often unwell and Joseph tried to be around for her. He even went shopping at odd hours when she had a sudden craving for strawberries.

Vishakha was forgotten. Then Flora went through a bad phase. Her gynaecologist was afraid that she would lose the baby and advised complete bed-rest. This meant that she had to spend long lonely hours at home with the maid, although Flora's mother, aunts, cousins, Sippora, Sharon and neighbours old and new spent time with her, often bringing food and having lunch with her. Then, according to tradition, Flora's mother took her home, as it would be easier to look after her. But Vishakha's ghost still hovered over Flora and she was not willing to shift to her mother's house. She only agreed when Joseph promised he would visit her every day and have dinner with them, unless he was delayed at office, was invited out by friends or had to attend a staff dinner. Reluctantly, she left for her mother's house, making arrangements with the maid to do the household work every morning and prepare Joseph's lunch box. Joseph did not give Flora any reason to complain. Flora was declared safe during the seventh month and she decided to have the eighth-month ceremony in her own apartment. After that, she would leave for her mother's house again.

Flora returned to her apartment to organize it for the ceremony. She also wanted to surprise Joseph when he returned home, as he was out hosting a staff dinner. Instead, Flora was in for a surprise when she opened the apartment door with her keys and saw that all the lights were on. She stood still, sensing there was someone in the flat. She was about to scream for help, assuming that thieves had broken in, when she heard Joseph's voice and realized there was a woman with him. Her eyes went around the drawing room and rested on a new addition on the wall, hanging next to their 'perfect wedding photograph'. It was a black-and-white poster of a nude male sculpture with hands folded behind his back. The name of the artist, Michelangelo, was scrawled in an oblique line over it with a quote, '...every block of stone has a statue inside it and it is the task of the sculptor to discover it...'

Flora stood at the door in her dowdy maternity dress, swinging her keys, and rang the bell till Joseph came to the door, followed by a reed-thin woman in a tracksuit. Flora guessed that it was Vishakha. They were cooking and she appeared to be a regular visitor to their apartment.

When Joseph saw Flora, his face fell. He was holding a wooden spatula in his hand, as though he was carrying a flag. Vishakha stood next to him. Spitefully, Flora noticed that she was bow-legged. She was wearing heels and her hair was piled in a topknot on her head. Flora saw that they were both wearing similar blue aprons. It appeared that Vishakha was soon going to move in with Joseph.

Flora felt her temper rising but controlled herself. She hung the house keys on the hook near the main door as Joseph rushed to hug her. Vishakha removed her apron and gushed, her red lips opening and closing like a goldfish, 'Oh hello! I have heard so much about you from Joseph. We were in the same school in Bombay and surprise, surprise, we met again at the gym. Did you see that poster of Michelangelo? Wonder if you have heard about him, maybe not? Well, last week I was in Rome and I thought it was the perfect gift for Joseph, since he has lost so much weight. It's simply miraculous. By the way, Flora—your name is Flora, right— would you like to have some pasta? I was showing Joseph how to make pasta, since he lives alone…poor dear. I thought I'd help, as it can be made in a jiffy.'

Flora, enormously pregnant, stood listening to her chatter and answered in a clipped tone, 'Are you inviting me for dinner in my own house? It is so kind of you to teach my poor starved husband how to cook, as he lives alone. Do you know, when he is not having these private dinners with you in our house, he has been having dinner almost every day with me at my parents' home, like a good son-in-law? And, as for pasta, this curry-crazy man eats pasta only with you. How dare you cook in my kitchen and invite me for dinner, as though it was your house, not mine! For your information, this is my home, not yours, so don't you even try to…'

Joseph put his arm around Flora, asking her to calm down, saying it was not good for her health. But she shrugged him off and, pointing to the door, screamed, 'Vishakha, that is your name, right? Get out right now.'

Joseph stood between the two women, feeling helpless, not knowing what to do. Vishakha picked up her clutch and rushed out, slamming the door.

Flora went into their bedroom without looking at Joseph, and opened her wardrobe while Joseph stood at the door, bleating, 'I am sorry, Flora. I should have told you…' Just then, the doorbell rang and Joseph jumped, afraid that Vishakha had returned to pick a fight, but Flora calmly went to open the door, mumbling that it was the maid. Joseph retreated to the drawing room, switched on the television, sat on his rocking chair and pretended he was watching the news. He heard Flora asking the maid to bring her bags from the storeroom and start packing her clothes. Joseph heard the maid ask, 'Why are we not cleaning the house and decorating it for the ceremony?' Flora did not answer.

Earlier, when Flora had turned the house key in the lock, she had planned to stay with Joseph till the ceremony. But when she entered the bedroom and saw the crumpled bedsheet, she was not sure but guessed that Joseph and Vishakha had made love there. Angry and humiliated, she had decided to return to her parents' home that very evening. As she packed, Flora listened to the maid's chatter, 'Since you left ... there was hardly any work ... used to come early to clean the house ... wash clothes and make Saab's lunchbox ... which he did not want anymore ... Often he gave me leave ... when he was touring ... I was just waiting for the day you would return home with your little prince...'

Flora changed the subject and asked, 'How do you know it is a boy?'

'I have three girls and a boy. I just have to see the way a woman walks and I know if it is going to be a boy or a girl.'

Once the packing was done, Flora had half a mind to call Sippora and tell her about her confrontation with Joseph and Vishakha, but decided to handle the situation herself. She called for a taxi, asked the maid to carry the bags downstairs and went into the kitchen for a glass of water. She was aghast to see the mess there and wanted to throw the pasta into the garbage bin, but stopped herself. She covered the vessel, went to the main door and, without looking back, made a grand exit saying, 'I am leaving.'

Quietly, she pulled the door shut, as she did not want the neighbours to gossip about their fight, although she was sure they knew about Vishakha's frequent visits to their apartment. By the time she reached her parents' home, she was in tears. She had called her mother and told her about Vishakha's presence in the apartment. Her mother was waiting at the door with open arms. Her father paid the taxi driver and carried the bags inside. In the comfort of her parents' home, Flora became hysterical as she told them about Joseph's lies and possible affair with Vishakha.

Her parents were in a dilemma, as they had already made an announcement in the Jewish community about the eighth-month ceremony. Eventually, when Flora calmed down, she called Sippora, who took control of the situation and persuaded Flora and her parents to go through with the ceremony as planned. 'No,' Flora said, 'not in Joseph's apartment, but here.' They would have to take Sharon into confidence and make sure that Joseph would be present for the ceremony. It would be their big secret.

Sippora called Sharon, who understood the problem. Both women informed the invitees that the venue of the ceremony had to be changed, as Flora was unwell.

On the day of the ceremony, Sippora and Sharon organized everything and dressed Flora in a bright pink embroidered sari with gold jewellery. Samuel had persuaded Joseph to be present and drove him to Flora's home.

Joseph arrived, looking dapper in a grey suit. Throughout the ceremony, he behaved like a loving husband. At the end, he had lunch with them and stayed till the last guest had left. Flora sat next to him, expressionless, like a statue.

Later, Sippora and Sharon took her back to her room and helped her undress. Unable to control her feelings, Flora slumped on the bed, sobbing. 'I feel sorry for this child. He will come into this world without a father.'

The women comforted her, saying, 'Come on, Flora, Joseph is a good man. It will pass…'

'Even if he leaves Vishakha, I will never go back to him. How could he allow another woman to sleep in our bed and take over my kitchen?' When she had calmed down, they left, wondering what the future held for the child who was about to arrive in this topsy-turvy world.

After the ceremony, Flora and her family did not see Joseph. But Samuel kept him updated about Flora's health and even informed him when she was admitted to the hospital, where she gave birth to a baby boy.

It was not an easy delivery. When Joseph offered to help by remaining at the hospital, Flora's father refused, saying that they would manage. Joseph called Sippora and apologized for hurting Flora. She listened to him, but kept silent, as it was for Joseph and Flora to decide about their future.

Sippora sensed that Joseph wanted to see his son. But their priority was Flora. She had mixed emotions and could not stop crying. And, when her parents said that according to the law, they had to inform Joseph about the birth of his son, Flora shook her head, saying nothing.

However, Prophet Elijah has his own way of sorting out the problems of his devotees. The Prophet intervened during the child's circumcision ceremony or Brit. The ceremony was to be on the eighth day after the child was born. As the child was weak, it was delayed for a month. During this period, Flora's parents, Samuel, Opher, Sippora and Sharon convinced Flora that the circumcision could not be held without the father of the child. Meanwhile, Joseph had sent a message to Flora through Samuel that he wanted to see his son. Flora agreed half-heartedly. By then Joseph had changed his mind and called Samuel to say, 'I think this is not the right time to meet Flora. She has just returned to her parents' place with the baby. I will be present for the circumcision ceremony at the synagogue.'

A date was decided. Joseph paid the airfare and hotel accommodation of the mohel who would perform the circumcision and had him flown from Mumbai to Ahmedabad. He met Joseph and Flora's father at the synagogue office and briefed them about the ritual. That evening Flora's father said to her, 'Joseph has changed.'

'How can you say that?'

'I cannot say how, but he has.'

The next morning, Flora met Joseph and helped him carry their son into the synagogue. She noticed that Joseph no longer resembled his old self, but looked more like the man she had first met at Sippora's place. He was fat and haggard, in misshapen clothes, with a kippa on his head and prayer shawl draped around his shoulders. She felt comforted that the child was with his father. It was then that Sippora stood next to her and whispered, 'It's over.'

'What?'

'Joseph's love affair.'

'How do you know?'

'Samuel asked Joseph and we came to know that he has broken up with Vishakha. When not at work, he is home. The maid cooks for him. He often eats at the office canteen or makes his own food ... misses you ... and, by the way, nobody knows about the affair ... so all is well.'

After the ceremony, when Flora's mother brought back the child, Flora took him in her arms, sat on a chair and fed him as the women huddled around her. They left when they saw Joseph standing in the doorway. He sat next to her and asked, 'Flora, have you decided on a name for our son? The naming ceremony will start in half an hour. Remember, we had decided on Simha or Shalom.' She nodded her head in approval.

Together, man and wife returned to the synagogue in a shower of confetti and bonbons. As boondi laddoos were distributed, the cantor said the prayers, blessed the child and named him Shalom. Joseph held his son and sobbed as Flora held them both in her arms. Feeling crushed in his parents' arms, Shalom let out a loud wail and the congregation burst out laughing.

14
Rose

Iт wᴀs ᴀ nightmare. Rose was standing holding her baby on the balcony of their third-floor apartment A-107 of Shalom India Housing Society, when she felt him slip from her arms. He did not fall, but unfortunately, at that very moment, her husband Enock came out to ask her to make a cup of tea and saw what happened. He was furious—Yehuda could have fallen to the ground below and died. He would have lost his son, whom he had received as a boon from Prophet Elijah. He snatched the crying child from Rose's arms and slapped her hard. Rose fell, struggled to stand up and tried to take the baby back, but Enock pushed her away.

Enock and Rose were new arrivals at the society. Enock had been transferred from Mumbai to Ahmedabad, where he worked in a well-known paint manufacturing company in the far western suburbs. With Ezra's help, they had rented Juliet and Romiel's apartment for a year.

Growing up in Mumbai, Rose was known for her beauty in the Jewish community. Enock was a distant cousin, a good-looking young man and a perfect match. He had been smitten by her from a young age. Against his mother Pearl's wishes, he had married Rose. Much before Enock had decided to marry Rose, like most mothers, Pearl had chosen another girl, Jacobeth, for Enock, and had been disappointed when he had fallen in love with Rose.

Pearl had expected that Rose would get pregnant within a year of marriage, but she did not. She gave birth to Yehuda only after five years.

From the first day, Rose noticed that Enock had a short temper. He was mild mannered with others, but generally bad-tempered at home. He had a tendency to get annoyed about small things like a badly folded shirt, less salt in the food or more sugar in the tea. She was always careful of his dark moods and tried not give him reasons to get angry. But this particular incident happened suddenly and she was caught unawares.

After she had got married, Rose suffered from vertigo for a while. She wondered if the ailment had returned, although her doctor had told her that she had been cured. She mused whether it was because of the rains. It had been raining continuously and the sky was laden with dark clouds. In a way Rose was happy, because the atmosphere was almost like Mumbai, after a long summer. Even the wilting money plant in the balcony had blossomed. There was no respite from the rains for days and the sun did not come out even for an hour. But that particular afternoon was windy and the clouds seemed to be parting, so Rose had decided to put some clothes to dry in the balcony. She was carrying the baby on her left arm and arranging the clothes with her right hand. It was then that Enock came looking for her. In a split second the baby slipped, although Rose was holding Yehuda in a tight grip and there was no possibility of his falling.

Rose had been tense since the morning. Enock had been in a bad mood and she had been expecting him to explode. He never talked about his office problems, but whenever she overheard him speaking on the cell phone to his colleagues, she realized he had a lot on his mind. It was a holiday and after his morning cup of tea, he had already asked her to make five more cups. Rose assumed that along with office problems, he also had acidity.

Rose again made tea for him, tears streaming down her face. She spent the evening crying, huddled in the bedroom, as Enock walked the length and breadth of the apartment angrily with Yehuda in his arms. The child was hungry and kept wailing. When Enock slumped on the sofa, tired of the child, Rose rushed and took Yehuda in her arms. Enock did not resist. Carrying the child, she switched on the gas, prepared his milk bottle, sat down in a chair and fed him till he fell asleep. She left him in his crib and made fried rice for dinner. Like a good wife, she filled a plate for Enock and left it next to him on a table in the drawing room, where he was watching the news. He ate and went out for a walk. Rose then ate, washed the dishes, changed into her nightdress and carried Yehuda to the bedroom, where she fell asleep holding him. Enock returned and sat in the balcony reading *The Book of Psalms*.

A week passed and Rose was worried, as Enock had stopped speaking to her. He accepted whatever she gave him—tea, breakfast, lunch box and dinner—but never asked for anything. He spent more time with Yehuda and like Rose, often slept holding him in his arms. On such days, he did not allow Rose to come near the child. When it came to Yehuda, there was a kind of silent tug-of-war between them.

Two weeks later, one morning, Rose heard the doorbell ring. She rushed to the door and saw through the peephole that Pearl was standing there with her bags. Rose opened the door and greeted her, but Pearl marched straight past her into the house.

As Rose went into the kitchen to make tea for her mother-in-law, Pearl woke up Enock, went to Yehuda's crib, picked him up and returned to the kitchen. When Rose offered her a cup of tea, she refused and ordered Rose to leave the house immediately. She shouted at her, 'Yehuda was a blessing from the Prophet; we do not want to lose him because of your carelessness.' She used abusive language and called out to Enock, asking him to push Rose out of the house.

Rose stood her ground and confronted her mother-in-law. She screamed till their neighbours had collected outside the door. They were whispering among themselves. In the presence of so many people, Pearl's grip on Yehuda loosened and he started slipping from her arms. Rose allowed the child to slip just a little, then quickly sprang forward and broke the fall and took Yehuda in her arms. She said to Enock, 'Did you notice that Yehuda was about to fall from your mother's arms? Now what shall we do? Should I call the police? Can I do what you did to me? No, I cannot, as I am your wife. But you and your mother can do whatever you like with me.'

Holding on to the crying child, Rose turned around and in a split second, opened the front door and faced the group of neighbours standing outside their apartment. They looked helpless; they did not know whether to interfere or help in such a personal matter. Rose told them exactly what had happened. She did not exaggerate as Enock would have done, but told them the facts and asked for help.

Salome was the first to come forward. She gave Rose a hug and led her downstairs to her apartment. The crowd parted as Rose walked out of the apartment with Yehuda in her arms, followed by Salome walking behind her like a bodyguard. By then, Ezra had arrived. His presence had a calming effect on Enock and Pearl. He advised them to cool down and stopped Enock from following

Rose as she went down to Salome's flat on the ground floor. Like a raging bull, Enock was still raring to drag Rose back into the house, but Ezra held him back, hoping that if the couple stayed away from each other for a few hours, the crisis would pass. Eventually, Enock invited Ezra and the others to his house for a cup of tea.

Pearl was annoyed at the turn of events. She had never been happy about Rose, as she was very beautiful and a good cook. So, when Enock phoned her and told her how Yehuda had almost fallen from Rose's arms, she had come to Ahmedabad determined to get rid of Rose forever from their lives. She did not know what she was letting herself in for. Though Rose looked delicate and had a slight vertigo problem, she was a woman of steel.

At Salome's home, Rose comforted Yehuda till he stopped crying and started dozing. Later, she gratefully accepted a cup of tea Salome made as she chatted with her. Rose's eyes were riveted on the opposite wall on the poster of Prophet Elijah in his chariot, flying to heaven. For a second, her eyes closed. She was half-asleep, half-awake and saw herself in a chariot fleeing from Ahmedabad with Yehuda in her arms.

At that moment, she decided to escape. She would take an autorickshaw to Kalupur railway station, catch a train to Mumbai and go to her mother's house. But she had left in a hurry, and did not have any money. She knew Salome would not help her escape, so she borrowed money from her on the pretext of buying tinned milk for Yehuda. Salome looked through her bag and pulled out a 500-rupee note. She hesitated, but Rose assured her that she would just go down to the shopping centre round the corner, buy the milk and return the change to her. She also told Salome that after buying the milk she would go back to her own apartment and face the consequences. Fortunately, she was dressed in a clean salwar-kameez and purple dupatta, almost the colour of the Prophet's robe.

Rose left Salome's apartment, took the stairs and walked out of the building towards the shopping centre. Then she took an autorickshaw to the railway station, bought a ticket for Mumbai and waited for the midday train, worried that Enock would track her down. She need not have worried, as he assumed that she was in Salome's apartment and would eventually return home by evening.

In the train, Rose found her seat and kept whispering a prayer to Prophet Elijah to convey her apologies to Salome, to whom she had lied. She asked the Prophet to give Salome the courage to answer Enock's questions about her disappearance. She had great faith in the motherly Salome, who would truthfully tell him that Rose had left her apartment to buy milk for Yehuda. Rose knew that Salome would silently thank the Prophet for inspiring her to escape.

When Rose reached Mumbai, she couriered the money to Salome, who later came to know that she had left for Israel with Yehuda. Nobody heard from Rose again.

15

Jennifer

JENNIFER WAS WEARING a bright yellow sari after a long time. Enock was surprised, as he had only seen her in white saris since her husband Elizier had died in a road accident, soon after Rose had left him. Elizier was a distant cousin of Enock, who lived in the far eastern side of Ahmedabad. The whole community had gathered at Elizier's funeral and they had all come together to help Jennifer and the children. After all, Elizier had not even been forty when he had died, leaving behind Jennifer, five-year-old Shirley and three-year-old Jonathan, who was a little older than Yehuda, Enock's son.

Enock regretted that he had allowed his mother Pearl to interfere in his life. Had he handled his own problems, maybe Rose and Yehuda would still have been with him. He ached for them.

When Elizier was alive, they often had family get-togethers or potluck on Sunday afternoons. Those were happy times. His eyes moistened as he remembered how Yehuda and Jonathan had played together like brothers. Shirley was very fond of Yehuda and often kept a watch on the boys while Rose and Jennifer prepared lunch. They frequently met in one house or the other, so that the families did not feel cooped up at home on holidays. It was better than spending the day in front of the television or an occasional trip to a gaming parlour at the mall. Enock became sentimental at the memory of those long afternoons they had spent together. After lunch, the women would lie down in the bedroom and chat about household matters, the children would doze next to them and the men would play cards or watch a cricket match on television. In the evening as a rule, the men made tea, much to the women's amusement.

Along with the Jewish community, Enock had organized the rituals following Elizier's death. The sudden death had come as a shock and Jennifer was unable to handle her personal loss and the legal formalities which follow a death, and that too an accident. She often called Enock about problems related to the accident, the police case and financial matters. He would help her by keeping the concerned papers and, whenever necessary, go to her place to get her signature.

For fear of criticism from the Jewish community or Jennifer's neighbours, Enock never stayed for more than half an hour. He made sure that the door was open, accepted a glass of water, asked about the children's well-being and left hurriedly.

Although he had convinced himself that he was not attracted to Jennifer, he was always worried about the gossip at the synagogue. When they met at community gatherings, a malida or a festival, he rarely acknowledged Jennifer's presence, even if the children came to greet him and ran back to hide in the folds of their mother's sari.

After Rose's sudden departure, Enock started having lunch at his office canteen and made an arrangement with Salome to send him dinner in a tiffin carrier, for which he paid. Sometimes, Salome also sent him lunch on Sunday or looked after him when he was unwell. She was more than happy to help residents of Shalom India Housing Society, as it brought in extra income. Her husband Daniyal got a paltry sum as messenger or Shamash of the Jewish community, for whom he also ran errands.

Enock was in a state of shock and not yet accustomed to living alone. His neighbours and friends were awkward about his new situation. And, as often happens after such unpleasant incidents, people kept away. But whenever he took an after-dinner walk in the garden of Shalom India Housing Society, they greeted him and stopped occasionally to talk about the weather, politics or rising prices.

After Rose had left him and Pearl had returned to Mumbai, Jennifer and Elizier had stood by him. It was with great relief that he received a phone call from Elizier saying they would visit him. And Enock's heart warmed when he saw Elizier and Jennifer standing in his doorway. For a while they avoided talking about Rose's sudden departure. Instead, they talked about his office problems. When they started discussing his arrangements for food, Jennifer asked casually, 'Have you heard from Rose?' That was enough for Enock to break down as he told them about the events which had led to their separation. Later, when Elizier and Jennifer were sure that Enock was better, they left.

A month later, Elizier died in a road accident. Although upset by the loss of a dear friend, Enock was supportive of Jennifer. When he saw her handle her tragedy with strength and fortitude, it helped him cope with his own life. He was impressed when Jennifer found herself a job as a primary schoolteacher.

Jennifer was not like Rose. If Rose was fair, Jennifer was petite and dark. She had also had a difficult past. It had not been easy for her to get married to Elizier, because she was not Jewish. Her real name was Surabhi. They had met in Mumbai, where Elizier had been transferred for a year. They had worked in the same office and fallen in love without thinking about caste, creed or religion. There had been opposition from their parents. But Enock had stood by them and helped them take the decision that Surabhi convert to Judaism. In the beginning, it had not been easy to convince her parents. Later, she went through a rigorous study of Judaism at a synagogue for three years and was eventually converted in a ceremony, in which she had become Jennifer. This was how Enock and Jennifer were connected through various incidents of their lives, including Elizier being Enock's best man when he'd married Rose.

In the present situation, Enock did not want the Jewish community to know that he was helping Jennifer. He told himself that it was just that their paths had crossed at strange turning points.

On New Year's Eve at the synagogue, Jennifer's yellow sari changed everything. Enock noticed that her dark skin glowed, and the colour was reflected on her cheeks. He did not recognize her at first, but when Jonathan left her side and ran towards him, entwining himself around his legs, he looked up and saw Jennifer. After the New Year's Eve prayers, when everybody shook hands, little Shirley stood at the doorway of the synagogue with a platter of apples and honey, with Jennifer standing nearby. On the way out, Jennifer walked next to Enock and asked, 'What are your plans for tonight? Nothing, I am sure. Why don't you join us for dinner?' Enock accepted her invitation and took them home on his scooter.

He felt it was a new beginning. As soon as he entered Jennifer's house, he was enveloped in the warm fragrance of fish curry. He remembered that both Rose and Pearl were good cooks, but had a different way of making fish curry from Jennifer.

Jennifer set the table with an extra plate for him and went into the kitchen to heat the food as Jonathan curled up in Enock's arms and recited a nursery rhyme. Enock found himself smiling after a long time. An old memory stirred and he felt as if he was holding Yehuda. He was sure that Jonathan missed his father as much as he missed his son. Little Shirley was also trying to climb onto his lap. He hadn't laughed this much in a long time, so much so that

Jennifer rushed out of the kitchen, asking, 'I hope the children are not bothering you?' She went back when she saw that they were all smiling.

In the kitchen, she wiped a tear and looked gratefully at the poster of Prophet Elijah above the Sabbath candle stand. She was moved that the children were playing happily with Enock, the way they used to with Elizier. She worried about Enock and wondered how he spent his time. At least she had the children. She often wondered if men and women handled tragedy differently. Although after losing Elizier she had passed through hard times, not knowing how she would live without him, on those days, Enock had always appeared at her door to help with the endless paperwork. He may not have stayed more than five minutes and sometimes not even entered the house, not accepting a glass of water or cup of tea, but she knew that he was always there for her since she had lost Elizier.

When Jennifer lit a candle for Rosh-Ha-Shana, they ate together like family. The dinner was excellent. Enock felt like he had not eaten good food in a long time. After dinner, Jennifer served the traditional New Year sweet chik-cha-halwa. Then she told the children to change and go to bed, as they had to go to school early next morning. They kissed Enock and disappeared into their bedroom as he helped their mother clear the table, a task he had never done with Rose. But Jennifer with her ready smile had put him at ease. As Jennifer had been on her feet all evening, Enock sat for some time in the drawing room and she sat across from him, telling him that she had celebrated the New Year for the first time after Elizier had passed away.

He was struck with remorse, as he had not thought about Elizier's family during festivals. Maybe he should have bought them gifts. So, when leaving, he thanked Jennifer for the New Year dinner and suggested that on the coming Sunday he would take the children to a nature park and they could have ice cream together.

That night, Enock returned home with a tune on his lips. Since Rose's departure, he had entered the apartment with a sense of remorse and often sat in the darkness, not knowing what to do, till he discovered that the television could be a good friend. So he would switch the television on even before he switched on the lights. He would zap various channels till he had dinner, freeze the leftovers, take a stroll in the garden downstairs and go to bed after the 10 o'clock news.

In contrast, his mornings were hectic, as the young boy who worked for Franco Fernandez in Block-B cleaned his apartment and washed the dishes while he made tea, toast and eggs for breakfast, bathed, dressed and left to catch the office bus. Food did not matter to him anymore till the New Year dinner at Jennifer's place. The fish curry worked like a magic potion.

From that night, he started fantasizing about the woman in a golden-yellow sari, serving him bright red fish curry over a mound of white rice. On some such evenings, Enock would switch off the television and start thinking about Jennifer. He wondered if he just needed another woman in his life, or was he longing for Jennifer's company? And since taking her and the children to the park, he was past caring about what the Jewish community said about his frequent visits to Jennifer's home, their occasional trips to the zoo or going to see a children's animation film at the cinema.

But being a woman, Jennifer was cautious and distant at the synagogue. Once in a while, Enock also had his moments of doubt. He worried about getting closer to Jennifer and making the same mistakes he had done with Rose. He had to pass the acid test. Once this doubt started nagging him, he stopped calling Jennifer. Unable to understand his sudden silence, she called him, asking if he was unwell. All he said was that his workload had increased in office and he could not see them like before.

After Enock started having mixed feelings, he retreated into a shell, not realizing that the children had started looking forward to his visits. They would call him, chattering away about their school activities, often snatching the phone from one another to recite a nursery rhyme. Enock told them that he was busy and would meet them as soon as he was free. He deliberately began distancing himself from them. He did not trust himself with another woman. He also avoided going to the synagogue for fear of meeting Jennifer. And, when he saw her there, he left hurriedly without meeting her. Enock had become conscious about comments being made by fellow Jews. They were all eyes and ears even if he looked at Jennifer and he was wary of their interest in his personal life.

With great difficulty Enock kept away from Jennifer for a little more than two months, keeping himself busy on Sundays. One such Sunday, soon after lunch, he was dozing and watching a cricket match on television when he heard the doorbell ring.

It was Jennifer. Uncomfortable with her sudden arrival, he put on a shirt over his vest and tried to tidy up the drawing room, littered with newspapers and teacups. Not knowing what to say, he blurted out, 'You are again wearing white. You look so much nicer in colour.'

She gave him a sad smile and said, 'White is what widows wear.'

'That was in the old days, not now.'

'Well,' she said, 'I was joking. But I wear white when I am sad.'

'Why?'

'Because of you.'

'Me?'

'Yes, we were becoming good friends and then suddenly, without explanation, you disappeared from our lives. This morning Jonathan and Shirley wanted to meet you. I wondered why you don't come to our house anymore, so I decided to see you alone and ask if there was some misunderstanding. I left the children with my neighbour and here I am.'

'Will you have tea or coffee?'

'I would like some coffee…'

Jennifer made coffee and they sat at the dining table, coffee mugs in hand, as she waited for an answer.

Enock said simply, 'Truthfully, I have a problem.' He smiled wryly. 'I am ashamed to admit this, but the more I see you, the more I feel attracted to you. This really frightens me, as I do not know how you will react to my confession.'

Jennifer's face tightened and she chose her words carefully. 'You think too much about our relationship. For me, you are just a good friend. First, you were my husband's friend, now mine. I am thankful to Prophet Elijah that you helped me with all my problems after Elizier's accident. And we enjoy going out together. If the Jewish community gossips about us, I do not care. So let us be good friends like before.' She smiled and stood up to leave. Enock offered to drop her home on his scooter. She accepted and waited in the drawing room as he dressed quickly.

As soon as Shirley and Jonathan saw him, they jumped with joy. He stayed with them for a while and returned home, feeling relieved that they could still be friends. Yet, they no longer met like before. But sometimes he took them out for ice cream or accepted Jennifer's invitation for Sabbath dinner or lunch on Sunday afternoon.

A year passed. By then, Enock was sure that he was in love with Jennifer and decided to take the risk of telling her. Expecting a refusal, he was cautious, as she had not given any indication that she was interested in starting a new life with him. Soon after, Jennifer invited him for New Year dinner as though it was the most natural thing on earth. He accepted her invitation.

That night, as they sat sipping coffee after the children had gone to bed, Enock leaned forward, placed the coffee cup on the table and said, 'Surabhi, I love you.' She burst out laughing. They embraced, kissed and decided to get married and return to Mumbai.

16
Lisa

WHEN LISA FIRST came to see Cyril, dressed in an organza blouse with a white skirt, he thought she looked like an angel. He started dreaming that maybe she was his soulmate who had suddenly appeared on the empty horizon of his life. That very day, he made a secret wish to Prophet Elijah and decided to offer a malida if he married Lisa.

Lisa was from Switzerland and spoke English with an accent. She was fair as a snowflake and had a bright, open face and emerald-green eyes. She was collecting information about the Jewish community of Ahmedabad and had been given his name from the organization she worked with. She was fascinated with Ahmedabad, but had a special interest in Jews.

Lisa worked for an organization that invited volunteers to work on their project to eradicate poverty in Gujarat. She had rented Juliet and Romiel's flat A-107 at Shalom India Housing Society for six months, which was now empty, as Enock and Jennifer had got married in a simple ceremony at the synagogue and lived in Mumbai.

Cyril was not a resident of Shalom India Housing Society, but lived in a house in western Ahmedabad with his parents Nissim and Eva. He was a prominent member of the Jewish community. He was the director of an ice-cream company, but had become a historian of the Jewish community by choice.

He was also a bachelor, since at a young age, he had rejected all the Jewish girls he had seen at the synagogue and told his parents not to look for prospective brides for him. They suspected that he might be in love with a non-Jewish girl, but he made it clear that he would not marry outside the Jewish community. His parents then suggested that he choose a non-Jewish girl, someone similar to him in nature, and she convert to Judaism. He again refused, as he did not believe in conversion. Finally, his parents let him be, saying that he was too intellectual and it would be very difficult to find a bride for him. So he remained a bachelor till the age of forty. Then Lisa appeared on the scene and suddenly Cyril was transformed. He wanted to marry her. But considering his high standards, he had to find out her faith and religion, as she kept telling him about the finer points of Buddhism.

Lisa had been attracted to India when she had joined yoga classes in Zurich. She had become an Indophile and a vegetarian. She had taken to Indian food and learnt to make a basic meal of dal, rice and vegetables. Lisa also loved Indian pickles and chutneys.

Like most Bene Israel Jews, Cyril ate meat during festivals when it was made kosher at the synagogue, while the rest of the year he was vegetarian, although once in a while he had fish curry or asked Elisheba to make kosher chicken for his family. In principle, like most Jewish families of Ahmedabad, he was vegetarian, as meat was not made kosher regularly at the synagogue.

To impress Lisa, when Cyril invited her for lunch, he told her that they were vegetarian and rarely ate non-vegetarian food. She was pleased when she saw that Eva had made paneer curry with parathas, which was one of her favourite dishes.

Lisa became a regular visitor to Cyril's house. As a rule, they met only when his parents were at home. Lisa became very fond of them and sometimes spent the afternoon with them, while over cups of tea, they told her the histories of Jewish families. Lisa enjoyed listening to these.

Gradually, she became part of the family and attended Sabbath prayers with them, had dinner and was present at most of the Jewish festivals they celebrated at home. Sometimes she visited the synagogue with Eva, where the women joked about a possible liaison between the lifelong bachelor Cyril and Lisa. They saw that he was interested in a woman for the first time in his life.

The residents of Shalom India Housing Society often saw Cyril's car at their gate when he came to pick up Lisa or drop her home. They were sure that their story would have a happy ending, like that of Juliet–Romiel and Enock–Jennifer.

Lisa's religion became evident when, on Yom Kippur, while Cyril was downstairs with the men and was adjusting his prayer shawl, he happened to look up at the women's gallery. He was surprised to see her standing next to his mother, looking very elegant in a white salwar-kameez, her head covered with a white scarf. His mother had not told him that Lisa was a Jew and was going to attend Yom Kippur prayers. Eva saw the question in his eyes, shook her head and twiddled her thumb to indicate that she did not know that Lisa would be at the synagogue. So he leaned towards his father and whispered, 'Did you bring Lisa to the synagogue?' His father looked up at the women's gallery and said, 'No idea.'

After the last prayer, the Shofar was blown and according to tradition, to break the fast, the congregation was served glasses of blackcurrant sherbet. Eva shook hands with Lisa and asked, with surprise writ large on her face, 'Are you a Jew?'

Lisa lowered her eyes and whispered, 'Yes.'

After the prayers, the community members met in the foyer of the synagogue and wished each other 'Chag samekh'. Cyril and Lisa also shook hands. Smiling broadly, Cyril said, 'I did not know you were Jewish.'

Lisa was embarrassed. She left hurriedly, saying, 'I am fasting. Salome aunty has made dinner for me. I will see you tomorrow.'

That night, Cyril and his parents sat at the dining table eating a simple vegetarian pilaf with the traditional Kippur-chi-poorie made with a sweet coconut filling and talked about Lisa's appearance at the synagogue for the Yom Kippur prayers. In her defence, Cyril explained that some Western Jews did not follow Judaism but the Day of Atonement awakened their faith. Maybe something like this had happened to her.

Cyril slept in peace that night with the knowledge that Lisa was a Jew. Maybe he was close to finding his soulmate. The next day he called her, wanting to meet. She said she was busy and would speak to him some other time. Cyril was annoyed but decided to be patient, assuming that she felt awkward talking about her personal life in the presence of his parents. A week later, he invited her for dinner at a restaurant. She accepted.

When he picked her up from the gate of Shalom India Housing Society, she was wearing the same dress she had worn when he had seen her for the first time. As they ate, between long silences, they spoke about sundry matters. Then, Cyril asked her about her Jewish background and said that he had been surprised to see her at the synagogue for the Yom Kippur prayers. Lisa lowered her head, not willing to meet his eyes.

Suddenly she looked up and said, 'Cyril, I am sorry I did not tell you that I am a Jew. Last week I knew it was Yom Kippur and as I had not told you and your parents about me being Jewish, I knew that I should inform you before surprising you at the synagogue. But believe me, it was the first time in my life that I decided to go to the synagogue. I thought that if I did not inform you, it would hurt you. So I thought I would tell you and your parents and then accompany them to the synagogue. But on the day I was going to call you, our group had to leave for a village near Ahmedabad and we returned almost at midnight, so I could not. I am sorry to have surprised you.'

Cyril listened quietly and then smiled to relieve the tension between them. He realized how keen Lisa had been to hide her Jewish identity from him and though he felt cheated, he did not let her know. He had read books about the Holocaust—maybe Lisa's family had suffered and she wanted to forget. He knew of many instances in Europe when Jews did not disclose their identity. Finally, he took a deep breath and said, 'I understand that you must have a reason for not telling us that you are a Jew.' He waited for an answer.

Slowly, she told her story: 'My grandfather is a survivor of the Holocaust. We do not like to talk about it. My mother is an American Jew and her family migrated to America from Russia. Both are non-believers and non-practising Jews. We do not like to talk about our Jewish background, so I turned to Buddhism as a solution to my conflict.'

'Then why did you attend the Yom Kippur prayers?'

'The credit goes to you for my change of heart. This is the first time that I went to a synagogue. When I came to you wanting to know about the Jewish community, I learnt a lot about Judaism and suddenly, on Yom Kippur, I decided to fast.'

'When I saw you in the women's gallery at the synagogue, I was surprised…'

'I was sure it would shock you. But it was a special moment in my life and I wanted to be alone with myself. I also got a prayer book in English from the synagogue office before I went to the women's gallery.'

'My mother is really fond of you and she was wondering why you did not tell her about your Jewish background.'

'When I stood next to her, I saw so many questions in her eyes. But I thought I would talk to her later, as I was moved by the blowing of the Shofar. I experienced so many mixed feelings that I did not know what to tell your mother.'

'I think they will understand if you tell them yourself.'

'Maybe I will come for dinner this Sabbath and explain everything.'

'Thank you. They will feel better if you tell them your story.'

As they parted, Cyril had half a mind to hold her hand and say, 'Will you marry me?' But he did not. Instead, he drove her to Shalom India Housing Society, praying fervently to the Prophet to fulfil his wish.

The following Sabbath, Lisa decided to wear a sari—a deep green sari with a red blouse. The green suited her eyes. But she draped the sari in a rather haphazard manner. When she rang the doorbell of Cyril's home, his mother saw her standing there, looking uncomfortable with the loose ends of her sari falling all around her. Eva smiled and asked Lisa to follow her into the bedroom. She taught her the correct way to wear a sari. In the process, she forgot the questions which were bothering her. Cyril had not yet arrived home from work.

His father Nissim sat in the drawing room, fuming, still annoyed that Lisa had hidden such a big secret from them even after they had welcomed her into their home like family. He was upset that she had possibly feigned ignorance about knowing anything about Judaism. When the women returned to the drawing room, smiling about the way Lisa had worn the sari, he frowned.

Lisa took one look at Nissim's face and froze. He sat with furrowed brows, neither smiling nor greeting her. Instead, he asked her a direct question, 'Tell me, Lisa, why didn't you tell us that you are a Jew?'

Lisa guessed that Cyril had not told them anything and, as he was late from office, she would have to handle the situation on her own. So she sat on the sofa between Nissim and Eva and told them about her background. She convinced them that though she knew she was a Jew, she did not know anything about being Jewish, the Hebrew prayers, rites and rituals. She was very grateful that she had learnt so much from them. It had helped her face the truth about her being Jewish. She was not sure if she would continue being religious, but they had helped open a closed door of her life.

When Cyril arrived, dreading to see the tension between Lisa and his parents, he was relieved to see them sitting together on the sofa, laughing and joking about Lisa's Jewish roots. He joined in their lighthearted banter and told Lisa that the sari suited her. He assumed that she had worn it to please him. He decided to ask her to marry him.

That night, his parents left them alone after dinner, hoping that he would propose to Lisa. Cyril offered to drop her back to Shalom India Housing Society, but as she was not in a hurry he said, 'Lisa, I like you very much. Will you marry me?'

For a second she looked stunned, then laughed nervously. 'You must be joking.'

'No, I am not.'

'Cyril, I really like you, but I cannot marry you. Next year I plan to marry my fiancé, Edward. He is finishing his doctorate in Zurich. Then we will settle in America. Sorry, Cyril. Now can you please drop me home?'

In that moment Cyril realized that Lisa was not his soulmate. And, after dropping her at the gate of Shalom India Housing Society, he returned home, determined that he would remain a bachelor for the rest of his life.

17

Sangita

YOU WILL NOT believe me if I tell you how difficult it has been to get to Ahmedabad from Israel. But here I am. This is my first trip to India. It's been such a long journey. It was really difficult, bahut mushkil. You may ask, if I have never been to India, how do I know Hindi? Arre … it was not difficult. I am an Indian Jew and have grown up on a diet of Bollywood films. In Israel, when we are not working outside the house, the CD player is always on and we watch all the latest Hindi films. Even if we are in the kitchen arranging the bartans in the dishwasher, putting clothes in the washing machine, drying clothes or running the vacuum cleaner, we may not be watching the film, but we follow the storyline through the dialogues.

Not that I understand everything, but by now I know most dialogues of old films 'by heart'. Maybe some day I will write my own script and send it to a film producer in Mumbai. I love period films, where the hero and heroine are dressed in flowing garments and take time to even hold hands. I like those films as the dialogues are simple and sentences like 'I love you' are said so elegantly, with a lot of tehzeeb, adab and mohabbat. All these beautiful words flow into me, they are part of me. Every time I watch a Hindi film, while doing a thousand and one things, my ears catch the sound of the words, which are sweet as honey to my Hebrew-attuned ears.

I am almost forty, but I am told that ever since I was a baby, whenever I heard Hindi songs, I would start dancing. That is why I was named Sangita, although Penina is my Hebrew name. I love the Bollywood 'jhatka'-style dancing so much that wherever there is a Hodu-Yada, an Indian event at Eilat in the south of Israel, I go to hear the music and songs from Hindi films. It stirs something Indian buried deep within me. Yes, I am a third-generation Indian Jewish immigrant living in Israel. I am ekdum hardcore Israeli. I have done two years of military service, like all young Israelis. I was even sent to the occupied territories as a soldier. I have lived in a kibbutz, picking oranges, washing dishes on industrial dishwashers while picking up dry dishes from the conveyor belt. I come from a religious family and was taught all the prayers, rituals and customs. I know them all. But now that I am forty years old, it is distant, as *'bahut zyada boring ho gaya…'* Now except for Bollywood numbers, nothing attracts me. And yes, I still need my monthly dose of chicken curry at my parents' home. Sometimes I get a craving for a samosa or sweets like pedas and gulab-jamuns. These are a must, but remain on the periphery of my life, because I am like any other Israeli woman. We work from 5 in the morning till almost 10 at night.

'Par ek din, meri life mein ek naya mod aaya…' Things changed for me. I was at my parents' home for Saturday lunch to be followed by the screening of a new Bollywood film on our television. But that particular day, my father became sentimental. Once in a while, he likes to tell me and my brother about our roots and family history. That afternoon he told us a story we had not heard before. It was

about our great-grandmother Penina. Till then, I did not know that I was named after her. Usually, he would become nostalgic when we started the fast of Yom Kippur or drove past the Ben Gurion International Airport at Lod, where the family must have first landed when they emigrated to Israel. Now that Pappa has grown older, he tends to slip into the past and become sentimental about India more often. Sometimes we listen, sometimes we don't. We keep shaking our heads automatically, half-listening or not at all, because the entire story is learnt 'by heart'.

Before I begin my story, let me tell you that whenever I introduce myself as Sangita, most Bene Israel Jews look down upon me almost with hatred, a 'nafrat ki aag'. I don't care, as I like to be known as Sangita. Well, aisa hai ki I am a divorcee… At a very young age, I fell in love … mujhe mohabbat ho gayi thi with my childhood friend Zev, that is, when we were in school. He is half-Israeli, half-Indian, half-Russian, half-Polish, half-half-half—but an absolutely gorgeous hunk of a man. And I am Indian with a Dutch strain from my mother's side, so I am fair and have auburn hair with blonde highlights. And, if you ask me about my divorce, *'Shaadi kyun break ho gayi?'* Okay, let me tell you. *Zev ko Indian food bahut pasand hai.* He loves Indian cuisine. A month after our fairy-tale wedding on the beach in Tel Aviv under a bright red canopy or chuppah, *mere sapne toot gaye jab usko pata chala ki mujhe Indian khana pakaana nahin aata.* He had thought that I know how to cook Indian food and was disappointed that I didn't. I bought Indian cookbooks and spent hours with my mother in her kitchen. I even watched food shows on YouTube and tried various Indian recipes, but I had no patience and was a failure in the kitchen. On my way back from work, I would bring falafel or borekas for dinner. And if I was in Tel Aviv, I would go to my favourite Indian canteen and ask them to pack tandoori chicken and naan, or a chicken curry. I made the rice at home, which would be either semi-cooked or overdone. I also made sure that whenever possible, Mother invited us to eat home-cooked Indian food. But he saw through my ploys and we were always quarrelling about small things. Gradually, I noticed that we had many differences and it was getting hard to make our marriage work.

Yes, I forgot to tell you that Zev worked as a technician at an aircraft factory and I worked as a cleaning woman at the airport. We did not spend enough time together and jab bhi we met, we quarrelled, till it started taking a toll on our marriage. Besides, whenever we were home, I would want to watch Hindi films, but filmy dialogues and teary scenes annoyed him. I would find that strange and ask myself, '*Agar usey Indian khana pasand hai, to phir usey Indian phillum kyun achi nahi lagti?*'

After three years of ladai-jaghda, one day Zev left me, saying that he was going to India. Soon after, I opened his Facebook page and saw he had posted his picture with a blonde he had met in Goa. Most Israelis love Goa. His new girlfriend had been living there for many years and was a surfing instructor. He returned to Israel with her after six months and asked for a divorce. So I agreed. *Maine divorce de diya. Phir uske baad main free ho gayi. Ab ghar jaa kar aaram se ek Hindi film zaroor dekhti hoon.* Then I decided to go back to university and became a fragrance chemist.

Now I no longer wash floors at the airport. I work in a company which makes perfume oils from minerals of the Dead Sea. I was happy with my new life. But all this came to an end, when my father told us about great-grandmother Penina. Yes, I was named after her. She was from Ahmedabad, Gujarat, India. Wiping a tear from his weather-beaten cheeks, he said that she was buried there and he had never returned to offer flowers at her grave. Unlike Israelis who place pebbles on graves, Indian Jews offer flowers.

This story hit me like a bullet. I thought I would forget it as I do my father's other stories, but I did not. I had a vague memory of seeing a sepia-tinted photograph in the family album in which she was sitting on a chair with hands resting on her knees, wearing a nine-yard sari and silver chains, bracelets, armlets, waistbands, nose rings, earrings and anklets. That afternoon, I found an old album in Mother's cupboard, studied my great-grandmother's portrait and realized with a jolt that we looked alike. But Father had told me that she was very dark, while I am fair. Whenever he spoke about her, he would say that she was known to be very progressive. She had joined a cosmopolitan ladies' club, played badminton and organized events to collect donations to buy medicines for the poor. I cannot imagine her playing badminton in skirts, but Mother explained that in those days, women tucked in their saris at the waist and wore canvas shoes. I was amused because I have worn T-shirts, hot pants, slit-denim jeans, sneakers or gladiator sandals for the major part of my life.

When, it comes to saris, *kabhi kabhi meri mamma sari pehenti hain*. Otherwise, she wears colourful blouses over trousers. *Skirts bhi pehenti hain*. Actually, I feel Western wear does not suit the Indian body—*acha nahi lagta*. But whenever we receive wedding invitations, *meri mamma Banarasi sari aur gold jewellery pehenti hain, tab woh bahut khubsoorat lagti hain*. But I do not know how to wear a sari. So for Indian events, I wear skirts, backless blouses, a dupatta and heels.

That month, after studying my great-grandmother's photograph, I decided to fly to India and look for her grave. For this, I did a lot of research. I even swallowed my pride and took my ex-husband Zev's help to work out a plan to reach Ahmedabad. He suggested, laughing, that I stop over in Bombay, as I am crazy about Bollywood. He knew it was the city of my dreams.

Eventually, I landed at Mumbai's Chhatrapati Shivaji International Airport. It was my first time in India, but I was comfortable. I went around the city in taxis and, peering out of the window, saw huge hoardings of the latest Hindi films and fascinating cutouts of my favourite actors. I felt I was in heaven. I stayed in a Jewish hostel and all went well. I could handle the traffic, the beggars chasing me and the spicy food. I became confident and befriended young American Jews living in the same hostel. We went around together and I felt safe. But I felt I needed my own vehicle, like in Israel. I was tired of taxis and autorickshaws. My friends helped me buy a second-hand car in a nice red colour. You won't believe this; I was comfortable driving around the city. So, like all Indians, I also started saying, 'If you can drive in India, you can drive anywhere in the world.' And I did.

During this time, I was in contact with my Pappa and decided to drive to Ahmedabad in my car. But he said that before reaching, I had to find a place to stay. He did not know anybody in Ahmedabad.

Anxious, I called Zev, who always comforts me; after all, we are childhood friends. He posted a message on Facebook about me. He pasted my photograph and wrote, 'Alone in Ahmedabad. This is my friend Sangita, whose Hebrew name is Penina. She is an Indian Jew from Israel. She is travelling alone. Her family has lived in Israel for the last three generations. She does not know anybody in India. Sangita–Penina Solomon is looking for her great-grandmother Penina Abraham Samuel's grave in the old cemetery of Ahmedabad. Can you help her? Please contact Sangita at her email ID…'

It worked. Two days later, when I opened my email, I had a message in my inbox from a member of the executive committee of a synagogue. It was a short mail but assured help. There was a cell-phone number I was to call on reaching Ahmedabad. I sent him a text message promptly, thanking him for his reply. He immediately confirmed the date and time we could meet at the synagogue. I was relieved.

By then, I was driving around Mumbai as though I had been living there all my life. My new friends were very encouraging. Every day we had lunch at the same café, where the manager gave me insights into Indian life and directions about the road to Ahmedabad. They advised me not to befriend strangers in a new city. But I was bindaas; *mujhe abhi tak aisa-vaisa koi anubhav nahin hua tha.* I'd not had any strange experiences. I had done a lot of shopping and had bought many clothes and knick-knacks as gifts for family and friends.

Close to my date of departure, the hotel staff got me a map and told me about the new expressway to Ahmedabad. I was excited about the journey to my father's motherland and was sure I would find my great-grandmother's grave before long.

I reached Ahmedabad late in the afternoon. But being a little impatient by nature, I had forgotten to ask my friends in Mumbai about accommodation. When I started looking for the number of the Jewish person from Ahmedabad, to my shock, I realized that I had lost it. I knew the number was in my laptop, but the laptop was packed in my suitcase, which was in the luggage compartment at the back of the car, under all my bags. That was when I ran into trouble.

The drive from Mumbai to Ahmedabad was smooth. I had been warned about traffic jams and that it took hours to reach the centre of the city. When I passed the toll plaza and reached the end of the expressway, I saw innumerable roads shooting out in all directions. Confused, I stopped my car and realized that in India it is important to speak a regional language, like Hindi. *Waise toh main thoda Hindi bol leti hun, par theek se aati nahi aur meri English bhi perfect nahi hai...* Both my Hindi- and English-speaking skills were inadequate.

I parked my car on the side of the road and started thinking of a plan of action. That was when I saw a paan shop and stopped to ask for directions. It had a small television screen, around which some young men were smoking while watching a cricket match. As I had not faced any problems in Mumbai so far, I rolled down the glass of my car window and asked the owner if there was a hotel nearby. When the young men heard my voice, they turned around, took a good look at me, talked amongst themselves, came towards my car and asked, 'New to Ahmedabad?'

'Yes.'

'From where?'

'Israel.'

'Great country, but you look Indian.'

'I am Indian.'

'Your accent is not like ours.'

I shrugged my shoulders.

'You have a lot of luggage?'

'Yes.'

'Follow us. We will take you to a hotel.'

I thanked them and waited for them to get into their car.

They looked like decent guys. I was tired and needed a clean hotel room to shower and sleep. They took a while to climb into their car. When they started their car, they gave me a thumbs-up sign and I followed them. That was a mistake. I could see from the changing landscape that we were driving towards a desolate area, where there was hardly any habitation, just street lights and dogs. At the expressway toll plaza, I had seen a list of emergency numbers, but had not thought it necessary to note them down.

I panicked when I realized that we were leaving the city behind and going towards a deserted area. I decided to confront them. We were driving side by side, so I rolled down my window and asked, 'Where are we going?' One of them stretched out his hand, held on to my window and said something nasty with a snigger. I immediately rolled up my window forcibly and drove ahead of them.

They chased me. I was terrified. But by then I had seen a sign which said 'Airport' so I drove at full speed. When I was sure that I had left them far behind, I drove towards the airport. I saw another sign in neon lights, which read 'Hotel', and stopped. Fortunately, the hotel was decent and I was given a good room with a view of the flickering lights of the newly built international airport. I wanted to file a police complaint against the young men who had chased me, but had no details about them.

I poured a glass of water from the jug, lay down on the bed and cried, feeling lonely and abandoned in a country which was not really mine. I needed to talk to somebody. Mamma would panic, Pappa would understand, but if I called him, he would worry himself sick and ask me to return to Israel immediately. Now that I had almost reached my journey's end, I could not possibly turn back. So I called Zev. He was concerned and comforted me, saying that such things happen and it was over now. I had to forget the incident, but not trust anybody from now on and avoid getting into trouble. When I told him that they were 'badtameez and bakvas boys,' he did not understand what I was saying and I could not find the equivalent Hebrew words. Anyway, he listened quietly and told me to order a strong cup of coffee and sandwiches.

Before we ended our conversation, Zev advised that I meet the contact person at the synagogue. I told him I had lost the number. He found it and gave it to me. I did as he suggested and the next morning, two members from the Jewish community of Ahmedabad came to meet me. They asked me to accompany them to Shalom India Housing Society, where they had made arrangements for my stay. I followed them in my car, which they asked me to leave in the parking lot, and carried my bags to an elevator in Block A, which stopped at Apartment 107. They told me that it belonged to Juliet and Romiel Abhiram, who lived in Israel. The president of the housing society, Ezra, had called Juliet and asked her to allow me to stay there for a few days. I looked around the apartment and saw a poster of Prophet Elijah in his flying chariot on the wall. We had a similar image in our drawing room in Israel. I asked him to help me find my great-grandmother Penina's grave. If I did, I would hold a malida for the entire Jewish community of Ahmedabad.

They had also asked Salome, an elderly lady living on the ground floor, to help me. I was surprised at how quickly everything worked out, as I was given a mattress, bedsheets, a quilt, a table, two chairs, a hotplate, an electric kettle and some pots and pans from people I had not yet met. Later, when I had showered and dressed, I received a phone call from the secretary of the synagogue saying that Salome's husband, Daniyal, would accompany me to the synagogue in an autorickshaw. I felt I was amongst my people, safe and protected.

The synagogue in the Old City of Ahmedabad was beautiful. It was exactly as I had visualized it. The artifacts, marble flooring, shimmering curtains embroidered with the Star of David, candelabras, chandeliers and soft light inside the synagogue elated me. After praying there, I was sure I would reach my goal. The committee members were friendly, and I was told the history of the Jewish community of Gujarat, and that there was only one synagogue in the state. Over endless cups of tea and snacks, I told them my family history and that my great-grandmother was buried in the old cemetery of Ahmedabad.

We spent the next day searching for her name in the tattered old logbooks of the synagogue. The president of the synagogue had advised that I should not drive alone in the city and suggested that I park my car in Juliet's unused parking space at Shalom India Housing Society. They made arrangements with a known autorickshaw driver, Babu, to take me around Ahmedabad, always accompanied by Daniyal or Salome.

It worked well. Daniyal and Salome were extremely helpful. I went with them to the graveyard in search of my great-grandmother. Salome always covered her head with her sari-end and I wore a sports cap. We spent four days looking for the grave. We read the inscriptions on each grave, which were written in Hebrew, Marathi and English. It was not easy looking around the graveyard. Although it was lined with trees, the land was uneven with an overgrowth of scrub and we had to walk carefully so as not to tread on the dead. Salome told me that the monsoon in Ahmedabad did not last long but sometimes, in August, the city received heavy rains and the cemetery was waterlogged. So every year, some graves sank deeper into the earth. It was very difficult to find caretakers to look after the cemetery and some graves had disappeared into the earth without a trace. Sometimes, when they buried someone on what appeared to be unused land, it was likely that by mistake, they were burying them over someone else. In the process, some graves could not be traced, even when the relatives of the dead came back year after year to look for them. The new cemetery on the far western side of the city on the banks of the Sabarmati river was better organized.

In a week, I realized that I had to give up my project of finding the grave in Ahmedabad. Gradually, I came to terms with the reality and decided to make the most of my trip. Since my arrival, I had been invited almost every day to one home or another for lunch, dinner or an elaborate Sabbath dinner. I felt my life was like one big party and, although I missed my family a bit, I dreaded returning to Israel. I amused myself by thinking that I could get married to one of the nice, highly educated, ageing bachelors of the Bene Israel community and settle down in Ahmedabad. To prepare myself for my imaginary life in India, I started learning to cook Indian food from Salome. She was a very good cook. Sometimes her friend Elisheba joined us.

Salome suggested that we meet in her apartment, as she had everything in her kitchen. All I had to do was buy some ingredients and vegetables. This arrangement worked well, as Daniyal was always away, running errands for the residents of Shalom India Housing Society and other Jewish families of Ahmedabad. He was also their messenger, as he went from house to house giving news of births, deaths, bar mitzvahs, weddings, engagements and malidas. His lunch hours were erratic, so the cooking lessons were held undisturbed, unless some woman from the society wanted to share a recipe or brought something she had cooked. In Salome's overcrowded kitchen, I saw many pots, pans and containers, which had come down to her from her family and Daniyal's. She had also collected a lot of kitchenware from other Jewish families, who discarded old vessels for new. Salome and Elisheba liked to collect these utensils for the various Jewish rituals they organized at the synagogue. I started photographing Salome's apartment and Elisheba's storeroom at the synagogue. I loved her masala box with its different compartments brimming with haldi, mirchi, jeera powder, mustard seeds and vessels of brass, copper, steel, bronze, tin, aluminium along with the plastic knick-knacks, which added colour to my images. Since my arrival I had been photographing the old Jewish cemetery, the synagogue and the Jewish women of Ahmedabad, dressed in a variety of clothing, saris, salwar-kameezes, skirts, flared pants and dresses, chatting, cheerful, having snacks in the synagogue pavilion, chopping fruits for the malida platter and meeting at the small office of the executive committee, where they discussed one ritual or the other. I also photographed them at prayer, especially during Friday evenings, on the Sabbath.

I was enjoying every moment of my stay in Ahmedabad. Once word got around that I was learning Indian cooking in Salome's apartment, it became the meeting place for the women living in blocks A and B. Even Jewish women living in the eastern or far western parts of the city came to share their recipes with me. Actually, every day, I had food which was delicious—lazeez, lizzatdar, behtareen and khushboodar!

The women of other communities from Block B also came to meet me. In fact, once we had a male guest, Franco Fernandez. He stood hesitantly at Salome's door, asking if he could come in. I knew him slightly, as while walking on the lawns of the society, I had often heard him playing his violin. Rather shyly, he asked if he could teach me how to make Goan vindaloo with chicken, as he knew that pork was taboo for Jews. So, we had a hilarious afternoon with Franco, who wore an apron printed with tiny piglets.

That evening, while passing by Salome's apartment, Ezra stopped to see what was happening. He was amused and suggested that I meet Juliet in Israel, as she was planning to start a restaurant. Far from Israel, it sounded very good. I felt like a bright future awaited me back home, as no ageing bachelor here had caught my eye. During this period, I had learnt to use a pressure cooker, something I had never used before. I had thought that it would blow up like a bomb. But nothing happened and I found that my food cooked faster than before. So I bought a pressure cooker and packed it in my luggage. My bags were overflowing and I was sure I would have to pay for excess baggage.

Then, much to my dismay, I opened my email one morning and realized that my date of departure was approaching. That night, teary eyed, I hugged Salome and informed her about it. I went up to my apartment, lit a candle to Prophet Elijah and thanked him for the wonderful gift he had given me of discovering India. Soon, all the residents of Shalom India Housing Society found out that I was leaving for Israel. Quickly, Ezra organized a farewell party for me, which was to be held on the lawns of the society where I had developed a passion for cooking and had met the wonderful people living in blocks A and B. This was the most beautiful memory of my stay in India.

For the party, I decided to dress in the typical Gujarati chaniya-choli with a flowing multi-coloured dupatta. I bought it from the Night Bazaar at Law Garden. It was a glittering dress with a backless blouse, to be worn with silver jewellery. Before the party, I went to a beauty parlour for a facial and hair spa. My hair had grown much longer than before, so I asked the stylist to dye it black. That evening, as I was dressing, I heard my doorbell ring. Pin in mouth and dupatta trailing behind me, I opened the door and saw Sippora standing in the doorway with a gift. I was as excited as a little girl when I opened the box and stood gazing at a beautiful sari. I felt I was holding a bowl of strawberries in my hand. It was a shimmering silk sari with a silver border. When the light moved, the colours mixed and merged into a bright strawberry pink, streaked with deep saffron. There was also a sari-petticoat and a ready-to-wear blouse. I caressed the silk and said to Sippora, 'I do not know how to wear a sari.' So, Sippora helped me tie the sari, as I made mental notes about the process. Then she combed my hair, rolled it into a bun and tied a string of jasmine flowers around it, so that I looked like a typical Bene Israel woman. I was ready to go to the party.

The youngsters of Shalom India Housing Society had arranged for a music system and, with Franco as their disc jockey, they played all my favourite Bollywood tunes, to which we danced till dinner was announced. It was a lovely party and I suddenly forgot all the Hindi words I knew. Everybody was talking in four languages— Marathi, Gujarati, English and Hindi. So I thanked them in Hebrew and bid farewell to my new friends.

I might not have found my great-grandmother Penina but I had discovered a new life that had seeped into my being. With these beautiful memories, I left for Israel. Before that I gave a cheque to Salome for being my food guru and left the car for her and Elisheba to start a food truck, which was their dream.

It felt strange returning to Israel. I had almost blanked out time and space. But I felt better when I met my family. I gave them gifts, returned to my tiny apartment and went back to work at the perfumery. But before that, I took my mother's old masala box which she no longer used. Along with the pressure cooker, it would have pride of place in my kitchen.

I reorganized my apartment with all that I had brought from India, and it started looking like an Indian home. I even hung six saris like a tent from my bedroom ceiling, so that I woke up every morning thinking of India. A month later, after I had settled down and returned to the rhythm of Israeli life, I was making Sabbath dinner for myself—dal, rice, bhindi that I had found in an Indian shop, with mince cutlets, when I suddenly remembered Zev. I had not thanked him for his support and help when I was in India. So, while cooking, I called and thanked him profusely. He cut through my sentence and asked, 'What are you doing?'

'Cooking Sabbath dinner for myself...'

'What are you cooking?'

'Dal, rice, bhindi and mince cultets.'

'Alone?'

'Yes.'

'Do you know how to make dal?'

'Yes.'

'How?'

'Magic.'

'Can I invite myself for dinner? I am half an hour away.'

'Sure, bring your blonde along.'

Before Zev arrived, on a sudden impulse, I wore the sari Sippora had given me.

When I opened the door for him, he whistled on seeing me in a sari and breathed in the warm fragrance of Indian food. He was looking good in a black kurta, jeans and Kolhapuri chappals. We stared at each other. To distract his attention, I asked, 'Where is your blonde?'

'Gone.'

He was impressed with the food on the table, which I served in thalis I had brought from India. I lit the Sabbath candles, like in the good old days when we were husband and wife. Suddenly, I felt his hand covering mine. We were holding hands and saying the Sabbath prayers together.

As we kissed, he held me in his arms and asked, 'Will you marry me, all over again?'

'Yes. *Hum tumhe dil de chuke sanam.*'

'What next?'

'Maybe start an Indian café with Juliet.'

'Yes, why not…'

Later, Juliet and I met in Israel. Before her departure to India, I sent Dead Sea cosmetics and mud packs for Sippora's beauty parlour and for the women of Shalom India Housing Society. Juliet and I became partners and we started two cafés, one in India, the other in Israel. To decorate my Israeli café, I made a collage of the photographs I had taken in India.

18

Juliet and Romiel

JULIET'S FRESHLY WASHED hennaed hair was spread on the pillow and Romiel's head was resting on it. He inhaled the cool fragrance of her shampoo and perfume. She smiled as his hand caressed her belly. She was two months pregnant and they were looking forward to starting a family. They had worked in various restaurants in Israel and saved enough to return to India and buy cooking appliances for the café they planned to start in Ahmedabad, as well as expensive gifts for both their families. They would select a location and hire an interior designer. They would hire staff for their café, where they would serve varieties of falafel. They would furnish their apartment A-107 at Shalom India Housing Society beautifully and lead a good life. Later, they would send their child to one of the best schools in Ahmedabad.

As they lay in bed discussing their future, Romiel played with Juliet's wedding ring and said, 'You have been working so hard that your hands have become rough. Now that you are going to

Ahmedabad, spend some time at a beauty parlour and pamper yourself with facials, manicures, pedicures and feel like a queen. You deserve it.'

She ruffled his hair and said, 'You also need to spend some time at a salon. Look at your hair.'

They kissed and lay side by side, wondering what the future held for them.

In the last few years, they had made some important decisions about whether they wanted to live in India or Israel, and had taken the Overseas Citizen Card so that they could live in either country. Eventually, they would settle in one of the two, depending on where their café would give them the best returns.

Romiel's hand rested on Juliet's midriff as he thought about how their first priority was the child. The news had come as a surprise—Juliet had gone for her regular check-up and the gynaecologist had announced that she was pregnant. During the bus ride home, Juliet had felt happy and elated as she looked at young mothers with little children with new eyes. She was in a hurry to share the news with Romiel. It was lunchtime and she knew his cell phone would be switched off, so she sent him a text message, hoping that as soon as he switched it on, he would receive the good news. But while turning the key in the lock of their apartment, she suddenly got cold feet, her palms started perspiring and she had misgivings about having a baby and also realizing their dream of having their own café. Late in the afternoon, when Romiel called back, excited, she relaxed. That night, when he arrived with a cake, like children they stuck a candle in it, lit the candle, cut the cake, fed each other and called their parents in India to give them the good news amidst much laughter. Later, they lit another candle and thanked Prophet Elijah for bestowing so much happiness on them.

They had dinner, took a stroll around the block, returned and slept in each other's arms, exhausted but happy. Whatever doubts

Juliet had had about motherhood disappeared by morning as the light filtered in through the double lace curtains. She woke up looking forward to the prospect of having a child. Romiel pampered her with tea in bed. By late afternoon, however, Juliet began to feel that she did not want to give birth to the child in Israel. She wanted to return to India. She needed her mother more than anything else.

At the time, Juliet was working as a sous chef at a seafood restaurant and had a bright future in the food business. She finished work early, went home after shopping for supper, cleaned the apartment, ate a light meal and went to bed. When Romiel returned from work, Juliet was watching television and waiting for him. As a rule, because they worked long hours, they did not usually stay up for each other. Romiel sensed that Juliet had something on her mind. She was heating a bowl of noodles in the microwave with tears running down her cheeks. She said, 'I want to go home.'

'Home?' he asked, holding her in his arms.

'Yes, home…'

'But this is home…'

'No, during the sixth month, I want to be with Mamma and have the baby in Ahmedabad.'

Romiel laughed. 'After so many years in Israel, home means Ahmedabad and you want to be with your mother for the delivery…'

That night, they decided that Juliet would resign from her job, pay the arrears and return to India. But, Romiel's contract was more complicated, as he was the chef for the Indian menu at a five-star hotel, so he would have to stay back in Israel for six more months and follow her later. When they were both back in India, they would start a new life; by then the baby would have been born. Snuggling together in bed, they decided the names of the baby and the café. If the child was a boy, they would name him Aryeh and if a girl, she would be Maayan. Their café would be known as 'Fun with Falafel', where they would serve varieties of falafel with Turkish coffee laced with cardamom. They had researched the eating habits of Ahmedabadis and had come to the conclusion that they would do well. Both were experts in making falafels with a slight Indian twist and would serve them in a platter, like a one-dish meal, with French fries, gherkins and lettuce. They planned to have their café on the popular S.G. Road, which connected the Ahmedabad highway from Sanand and Sarkhej to Gandhinagar. They had been told by friends and family that all the eateries on this stretch did very well. They asked Ezra to send them details of possible sites to start their dream project.

Before Juliet left for India, whenever she had time, she made a variety of sauces to seduce Indian tastebuds, along with the typical green and red Israeli sauces. She was pleased when she hit upon the idea of making sweet mango chutney with ripe Alphonso mangoes and a tangy chutney with raw green mangoes. She had discovered that some agencies sold frozen mango pulp, and raw mangoes were available all year round. With her innovative mind, she would spice these up and create her own exotic version of Indo-Israeli chutneys. Juliet was excited by the thought that she would conquer Ahmedabad's falafel market. Both she and Romiel were already well known in Israel for their falafel and Indian curries.

According to Israeli regulations, as Romiel was in his thirties, he was a reserve soldier, so there was always the possibility that he would be called to serve in the army. Both Romiel and Juliet had prepared themselves for this eventuality.

During the week of her departure, Juliet decided that she would not return to Israel again. One afternoon, she made chai for herself, lay down on the sofa chair and took a nap. She woke up with a start as she heard sirens. The glass panes of their windows rattled and she saw a huge flare of light. It was as if a meteor had hit their building, followed by a huge booming sound, as if a hundred tanks were rolling down the street below. It was a missile launched from the Iron Dome Missile Defence System to destroy the rockets aimed at Israel. Juliet immediately picked up her runaway bag with her passport, medicines and a bottle of water and ran down to the basement bomb shelter, also known as the strongroom of their building, where she stayed with her neighbours and their children.

Since the time Juliet and Romiel had arrived in Israel, they had finished a course in Hebrew at an ulpan in south Israel, where new immigrants were housed. From there, a social worker from the immigration department helped them find jobs in cafés and restaurants. They had worked hard, from early morning to late night, and eventually decided to settle in Ashkelon by the sea. From their fourth-floor apartment, they could see the turquoise-blue Mediterranean Sea, cutting along the sky like a sharp blue line, so serene, so beautiful and so peaceful. On some nights, they sat in their balcony, watching the two dark masses of sea and sky, gazing at the stars and listening to the waves. On full-moon nights, they never missed their late-night rendezvous. It was then that they forgot all their worries and day-to-day tensions and felt at peace, wrapped in the cocoon of their private world. But on that particular night, a week before Juliet was to leave for India, she felt her world had shattered. Although the airlines were operating as usual, Juliet and Romiel decided that she would fly to India before the scheduled date.

On the day of the flight, Juliet went through the procedures like one in a trance and, like a zombie, reached Ahmedabad's Sardar Vallabhbhai Patel International Airport, where her parents were waiting for her. As soon as she hugged her mother, she wept as though she had lost everything. She regretted her decision to return to India. In her mother's house, whenever the phone rang, she started. She watched the news about the conflict in Israel and dreaded the worst. Although she knew that Romiel was used to the situation, he would not be able to leave Israel unless there was peace.

The conflict lasted fifty days and those were the most difficult days for Juliet and their families. As planned, she did not go back to her apartment at Shalom India Housing Society but stayed with her mother in her old room, sometimes chopping vegetables, sometimes cooking, trying out a new recipe and zapping television news channels. Her nerves were on edge, although her gynaecologist had asked her to relax and exercise. Eyes brimming with tears, she told her gynaecologist that all she wanted to do was curl up and die. She was immediately sent to a therapist, who tried to divert her attention to other matters. Besides sending her to a yoga class for pregnant women, where they did regular exercises, she suggested that Juliet listen to music and get involved in activities like painting greeting cards or learning a new craft. It helped her wait for Romiel. Juliet would keep visualizing her reunion with Romiel at the Ahmedabad airport, when he would arrive with a happy smile. But that was not to be.

On the fiftieth day, when the conflict in Israel ended, Juliet received a message, which was also relayed in the media: *We mourn the passing of a civilian, Rahul Romiel Abhiram, of Indian origin, aged thirty-two years.*

Acknowledgements

Thanks to all the Jewish characters I have created through the years. They stay close to me, like an extended family, and have reappeared in *Bombay Brides*.

While researching for my earlier novels, I had noticed that most Bene Israel Jewish men of Ahmedabad are married to brides from Mumbai. I would like to thank my publisher Krishan Chopra for his insights that helped me explore this theme. My thanks to Mala Dayal for editing this book, along with Amrita Mukerji, who was in continuous conversation with me, asking innumerable questions about my characters and illustrations, so that Bonita Shimray could design a striking cover. To Anand Zaveri of Swati Snacks, Ahmedabad, for making it possible for me to write *Bombay Brides* while sitting there almost every afternoon and to Somnath Chatterjee who solved my laptop problems.